ALPHONSE E[...]
his career letters i[...]
Les Hirondelles, [...]
by Victor Hugo, and, the same year, the historical melodrama, *Le Magicien*. This was followed, in 1840, by the novel *Charlotte Corday*, and again in 1840, *L'Évangile du people* [The People's Gospel], for which he was fined 500 francs and imprisoned for eight months at Sainte-Pélagie. He was elected to the Legislative Assembly of the Second Republic following the Revolution of 1848, and subsequently exiled from France following Louis-Napoléon's *coup-d'état*.

BRIAN STABLEFORD'S scholarly work includes *New Atlantis: A Narrative History of Scientific Romance* (Wildside Press, 2016), *The Plurality of Imaginary Worlds: The Evolution of French roman scientifique* (Black Coat Press, 2017) and *Tales of Enchantment and Disenchantment: A History of Faerie* (Black Coat Press, 2019). In support of the latter projects he has translated more than a hundred volumes of *roman scientifique* and more than twenty volumes of *contes de fées* into English.

SNUGGLY BOOKS

ALPHONSE
ESQUIROS

THE
ENCHANTED
CASTLE

TRANSLATED
AND WITH AN INTRODUCTION BY
BRIAN STABLEFORD

THIS IS A SNUGGLY BOOK

ISBN: 978-1-64525-053-1

CONTENTS

INTRODUCTION

"LE CHÂTEAU ENCHANTÉ" by Alphonse Esquiros (1812-1876), here translated as "The Enchanted Castle," first appeared as a four-part serial in the weekly periodical *L'Artiste* between 6 September and 27 September 1846, and was reprinted in its entirety in the October 1846 issue of the monthly *Revue de Paris*. The short story included with the novella as a makeweight, "Ebn Sina," first appeared in the 13 July 1849 issue of *L'Artiste*. Both stories were reprinted in a collection of stories and essays from *L'Artiste*, *Le Château Enchanté* (Dentu 1877), with an introduction by Arsène Houssaye, the editor of the periodical.

Esquiros' literary career was abruptly interrupted not long after the publication of "Ebn Sina" when he was elected to the Legislative Assembly of the Second Republic following the Revolution of 1848, and subsequently exiled from France following Louis-Napoléon's *coup-d'état*. The story illustrates, however, that he was already changing the direction of his thought and effort, and the other works he produced immediately before and during the brief interim of the Republic were even more stridently propagandistic. He had always seemed more comfortable when writing non-fiction, and his fiction had always tended to the didactic, especially when it was at its most fantastic. He enjoyed a long career as an activist on the far left of French politics, always an outsider, even under the Third Republic formed in 1870, when he was able to return to his homeland; he was elected to parliament again, but did not long survive his appointment as a Senator in 1876. In 1847 he married the feminist writer and activist

Adèle Battanchon (1819-1888), in collaboration with whom he wrote a curious exploration of the legendry of amour, *Histoire des amants célèbres de l'antiquité* [The Story of the Celebrated Lovers of Antiquity] (1849), and who continued to sign herself Adèle Esquiros long after their separation in 1850.[1]

During the reign of Louis-Philippe, Esquiros had been part of a group of politically active writers who were strongly affiliated to the Romantic Movement, and he was acquainted with most of the leading members of that movement, especially

---

1 Among the works by Adèle Esquiros reproduced on *gallica* is a volume of short stories. *Les Amours étranges* (1853); it includes an advertisement for a volume entitled *Le monde à l'envers* [The World Turned Upside Down], which does not appear to exist; whether it was not actually written or suppressed by the Second Empire's censors is anyone's guess. Although the couple separated in 1850 both contributed to a short volume published in 1859 with no ensemble title, in which the first story, "Une vie à deux," bears Alphonse's by-line, while the others, including "La Nouvelle Cendrillon," have Adèle's.

the younger ones. His first book had been a volume of Romantic poetry, *Les Hirondelles* [Swallows] (1834), written under the influence of the contemporary *cénacles*, which was extravagantly praised by Victor Hugo. It was swiftly followed by his first novel, *Le Magicien* (1834), a historical melodrama featuring both diabolism and alchemy; his second, *Charlotte Corday* (1840), exhibited his political inclinations and his strong interest in history much more obviously. When he became a regular contributor to *L'Artiste*—then a covertly radical periodical under the perennial careful scrutiny of the censors—Esquiros had already served a term of imprisonment in 1840, after publishing *L'Évangile du people* [The People's Gospel], an account of the life of Jesus that represented him as a social reformer, which was deemed to be an insult to religion.[1] All of his later writings were non-fiction, many

---

1 The judgment is an insult to the book; Esquiros was devout, but considered that the ideals of the Gospel had been betrayed by the Church.

of them produced in England, where he obtained somewhat ironic employment during the longest phase of his exile as a professor of literature at the Royal Military Academy at Woolwich.

It is possible that "Le Château Enchanté" was initially intended to be a novel and that the curiously synoptic style of its later chapters resulted from a belated decision to cut it short and wind it up; if so, it seems probable that the beginning of the story was first penned long before its publication, perhaps before *Le Magicien*, some of whose psychological fascinations it shares, and that it was taken up again belatedly by virtue of Arsène Houssaye's encouragement. Whether that is so or not, it is interesting that the novella was followed by a much more elaborate study of amour in *Histoire des amants célèbres de l'antiquité*, which provided a complement of sorts to the philosophical analysis carried out in "Le Château enchanté."

That analysis was followed even more rapidly by a very different complement, a scholarly essay in the *Revue des Deux Mondes* in 1847 on "Maladies de l'esprit; des idiots et des travaux récents sur idiotie," [Mental Illnesses; idiots and recent works on idiocy], which demonstrated a keen interest in and considerable knowledge of the pioneering work being done at the time in the "clinical asylums" of Paris, as well as offering a history and analysis of the concept of "idiocy," and a commentary on the possibilities of treatment. The article concludes: "To extract mental being from a void is the goal that God proposed himself at the commencement of the world when he said to himself: 'Let us make man!'"[1] The article makes no mention of mesmerism or magnetism, but it makes it clear that the process of psychological evolution imagined in the novella was a serious item of philosophical speculation.

1 *Revue des Deux Mondes* 1 Avril 1947 p.316.

There is a curious literary reference to Esquiros in Théophile Gautier's short story "Le Pipe d'opium" (tr. as "The Opium Pipe"), first published in *La Presse* in 1838, which describes how the author, after smoking opium with his fellow writer Alphonse Karr, has a dream in which he evokes "my comrade Esquiros the magician" in order to seek an explanation of his vision, and is hypnotized by the latter's "flamboyant and radiant eyes." Although the reference might simply have been inspired by Esquiros' first novel, it is highly probable that Gautier was well aware of his friend's interest in abnormal psychology and mesmerism. Gautier and Karr both had an interest in *contes de fées* and experimented with writing stories that transfigured such tales, much as the fundamental motif of "Le Château enchanté" does, adding further support to the supposition that Esquiros' novella might have been commenced in the 1830s under the influence of discussions in one of

the Romantic *cénacles* of that period—probably Victor Hugo's salon, in which Arsène
Houssaye first encountered Esquiros.

"Le Château enchanté" is a hybrid transfig-
uration, combining the key motif of the story
nowadays known in English as "The Sleeping
Beauty"[1] with the legend of Pygmalion and
Galatea, and carefully including further analogies to the story of Orpheus and Eurydice (one
of the legends subjected to close scrutiny in
Histoire des amants célèbres de l'antiquité) and,
most significantly, to the account of creation

---

1 The story is nowadays credited to Charles Perrault,
but the pattern of Perrault's first collection suggests
strongly that most of the stories in it, including "Le
Belle au bois dormant," are adaptations of stories read
aloud in a salon hosted at Louis XIV's court by the
dowager Princesse de Conti. The story—the second
part of which is omitted from modern recyclings—employs several motifs employed by Madame d'Aulnoy,
whose *contes de fées* were among those denied licit publication, probably by the influence of the Church, and
not printed (whatever reference books allege) until after her death; she is likely to have been its true architect
in that context.

given in *Genesis*. Given the nature and range of those fictitious references, it is tempting to consider the novella's employment of mesmerism as a literary device, not to be taken too literally, like the symbolic employment of alchemy in "Ebn Sina," but it is worth noting that Esquiros was by no means the only member of the French Romantic Movement to take serious interest in the uses being made of "magnetism" by the alienists of Paris; *Le Roman de l'avenir* (1834; tr. as *The Novel of the Future*), by the radical political activist and reformed Romantic Félix Bodin includes an exemplary fragment of a hypothetical novel of the future, which assumes that in the twentieth century magnetic medicine will have become an orthodoxy displacing other forms of treatment; and the most prominent clinical mesmerist of the period, the self-styled Baron Dupotet de Sennevoy (1796-1881), was an enthusiastic proponent of the notion that ancient magic was merely applied magnetism.

Although "Le Château enchanté" might appear in retrospect, therefore, to be something of an oddity—and all the more interesting in consequence—it was not out of keeping with the temper of its era, especially if it is assumed to have been planned and mostly written in the 1830s rather than the 1840s.

If its various layers of narrative flesh are stripped away by critical dissection, the fundamental anatomy of the story told in "Le Château enchanté" is not merely typical of the fiction of the Romantic Movement but archetypal, unusual only in its extremism. Extremism was, however, part and parcel of the Romantic quest, and it is not hard to find similar examples of calculated extravagance in the works of writers who were undoubtedly known personally to Esquiros, the most evident examples being displayed in the work of Théophile Gautier and that of the doyen of the *cénacles*, Charles Nodier. The climactic scene of Esquiros' novella is similar to the consummation of more than one story by Nodier, most obviously "Amélie" in *Souvenirs de jeunesse, extraits des mémoires de Maxime Odin* (1832; the cited story is tr. in *The Memoirs of Maxime Odin*). Although the modern commercial genre of "romantic fiction" is drastically diluted in its pretentions, and carefully vulgarized, fugitive echoes of classic Romantic extremism still persist therein.

As an exemplar of the original core of Romantic prose fiction, therefore, "Le Château enchanté" is as remarkable for its purity as it is for its flamboyance. It is, of course, rationally incredible, but that is not a bad thing in context, and might even be held to be a superior virtue. If the story was, in fact, commenced in the early 1830s and then abandoned temporarily, that would not be very surprising, given the subsequent shape of the author's career, but there can be no doubt that if Arsène Houssaye was responsible for encouraging the author to take it up again, he showed excellent judgment, and did readers a favor by allowing a truly remarkable literary specimen to see the light.

The translations were made from the copy of the 1877 Dentu collection reproduced on the Bibliothèque Nationale's *gallica* website.

—Brian Stableford, April 2020

THE
ENCHANTED
CASTLE

I

FOR nearly nine years one of the most beautiful houses in the faubourg Saint-Germain remained uninhabited.

Its shuttered windows only opened once a month in order to let air into the vast apartments. On that day, an aged domestic shook rich carpets and tiger skins at the windows, from which clouds of dust escaped. The courtyard was silent; a few parasitic sparrows pecked seeds of oats or blades of grass between the paving stones; spiders spun their webs between the idle wheels of carriages garaged there. There was solitude in all its sadness.

It has not always been thus; that house had once had its days—or, to put it better, its nights—of festivities, during which the shadows of young duchesses in low-cut gowns, with flowers in their hair, could be seen from the street passing over the misty transparency of the curtains.

But one evening, all the torches, candelabra, aureoles of fire, noises, music, bursts of laughter and foolish conversations on the balconies were suddenly extinguished. The street, illuminated until then by the reflection of its radiant soirées and lined all along its length by a row of rich carriages with blazoned panels, had taken the example from the other streets of the noble faubourg of silence and obscurity.

It was thought at first in the neighborhood that the owners of the house had gone to spend the summer on their country estates; they had, in fact, departed as usual one day in May, saying that they would return in the autumn, but the leaves had fallen from the trees into the courtyard of the house eight times since then, and the owners had not come back.

That prolonged absence gave rise in society to a host of conjectures. It was thought at first that an irreparable misfortune must have struck the noble emigrant family in the country, but no disastrous news had been received. Others were inclined to think it ruined, but the fortunes of the household had held firm for half a century against revolutions and civil wars with such an inexhaustible abundance that excessive expenditure, gambling and even the devouring follies of Parisian luxury would not have succeeded easily in eroding it.

The most curious interrogated a domestic who was worn away in that solitude, like the other furniture of the hotel, by lack of service; but, whether it was truly ignorance or discretion on his part, he only replied that he did not understand the conduct of his masters at all.

In the neighborhood, people remembered most of all a little brown-haired girl who had often been seen running, her hair in braids and her legs bare, under the tall chestnut trees that shaded the courtyard. They thought they could still hear her pretty voice, embarrassed by a slight stammer. According to the calculations of the local people, she must now be seventeen years old.

Her absence, at an age when serious thought ought to have been given to her introduction into society, excited increasing astonishment and curiosity.

What was the family doing in the country, then?

II

THE kind of life that it was leading in its château was scarcely less surprising. That château was situated in the depths of the Berri, on a small hill. One climbed up to it, by an oblique winding path, as sinuous and twisting as a snake. Its roofs outlined against the sky five slate-lined cones surmounted by weathervanes and large leaden trefoils. Seen from a distance, with its somber turrets and massive flanks, it was a building of severe taste. In addition to the fact that its architecture testified to a great antiquity, the château bore for chevrons vast cracks in its walls, aged by service. Swallows and wild pigeons built their nests in the fissures between the stones.

The château overlooked a thickly-wooded park, which masked the façade completely. The rear of the building was covered by high walls, gables, turrets and a few recent masonry-works of the last century, fitted into the ancient ones in order to fortify them.

The entrance door, guarded to either side by two dilapidated towers threatened by ruin, was studded externally by large nails with round heads. It displayed proudly on its worm-eaten panels the feet of wild boars, the antlers of deer, the heads of owls and the wings of kites, whose feathers had fallen into decrepitude. Those insignia of huntsmen had been fixed to the wood of the door by ancestors of the family, for the present master of the château did not devote himself to any of the violent exercises with which the rich proprietors of our day still try to break the monotonous uniformity of provincial life.

Nothing was sadder, to judge by the surroundings, than that habitation of the family de B***. That château, to which the return of the masters had brought back the luxury and tumult of Paris in spring every year, now seemed utterly abandoned. The bleakest and most eternal solitude imaginable reigned around its walls. The avenue planted with elms that led to the gate of the park had covered its old fine gilded sand with a layer of grass; the conduits charged with furnishing water to the basins refused their service, and part of the walls had fallen into ruin without anyone giving any thought to repairing them. However, the prolonged sojourn of the owners ought to have contributed to the good upkeep of the house.

Here, as in Paris, there was speculation about that extraordinary conduct. The idle life of the province invited a thousand curious and malicious comments, but the local landowners were no more able to penetrate the mystery than the neighbors in Paris to penetrate the secret of such a well-immured life.

No stranger was received at the château. Even the farmers who had to negotiate with their master never entered the interior of the building. The comte gave them audiences on the drawbridge. We have, in fact, forgotten to say that the body of the edifice was guarded throughout its perimeter by a broad ditch, into which the gutters of the house emptied when it rained. That was the only water it received, since the conduits, blocked or cracked by virtue of the negligence of the masters, no longer carried water there from springs.

The comte stood stiffly. He greeted his people with a cold politeness. His speech was curt and sparse. A cloud of somber sadness spread over his uncovered forehead and his sunken eyes, leaving impenetrable to everyone the secret of a dolor that doubtless lacked any consolation, since the wealth, the command and ever-increasing prosperity of his domains could not soothe it in the slightest.

Those farmers were, very nearly, true vassals with regard to respect and submission. The locale, still very little traversed by roads, travelers and newspapers, had not thus far opened to the revolution the means of penetrating it. That justified the title of *seigneur* that we shall have occasion to give to the owner of the château in the continuation of this story. There was, in consequence, nothing to fear from witnesses so mute and so passive; those people respected the comte's dolor instinctively, like children who avoid laughing and making a noise around their mother when they see that she is sad.

Apart from the brief interviews required by business affairs, Monsieur de B*** had no commerce with anyone in the locality. He lived alone, mysteriously. Around the château, so well defended by its thick walls and its foliage, the profound and particular silence extended that only falls around great misfortunes.

The curiosity of the region, like that of the city, fell principally upon the comte's daughter, a beautiful child who had once been shown off proudly, and who had suddenly disappeared. Might smallpox have disfigured her? Might she have become over time, by chance, a repulsive monster whom no one dared any longer to expose to gazes for the sake of the honor of the family? Might she have committed one of those sins against mores that, in certain ancient and austere families, draws after it an eternal mourning? No one knew.

III

THE nature of the Berri, which we visited two years ago, is grandiose and simple; it conserves a primitive character that the hand of civilization has not yet effaced, and which is found hardly anywhere else in France. The woods there are rarely pierced by roads; in certain places the difficulty of transport even protects their virginity against the offenses of woodcutters. Hills negligently crowned by wild trees, reddish ocher in the flanks of rugged mountains and idle streams lost under tresses of old willows or inclined birches, the waters of which are not fatigued by bearing heavy barges, all imprint on that solitary countryside a majestically calm air that engenders meditation; the absence of humans and their works generates thoughts of God.

That virgin nature marries marvelously with the ruins with which the region is strewn in several places; it seems that feudalism crumbled there yesterday; the remains of fortified castles, confused masses of detached stones, in the middle of which a somber keep still raises its bleak and discrowned head, mingle harmoniously with sheer rocks and impenetrable black forests. The wars of the Fronde have imprinted the trace of their iron fingernails on the proud feudal dwellings of which the genius of Richelieu completed the destruction or humiliation.[1] A few, however, have remained solidly seated on their unshakable foundations; enveloped in their solitude and their walls like a vanquished warrior in his cloak, they dominate the picturesque heights of the Berri.

1 The series of civil wars known as the Fronde, which raged between 1649 and 1653 occurred after the death of Cardinal Richelieu, so it was his successor, Cardinal Mazarin, who actually completed the process of cementing the power of absolute monarchy and stripping the nobles of their traditional rights to govern independently.

Mores have retained something Medieval, especially in certain ancient families which refuse obstinately all contact with the outside world; nevertheless, it is true to say that today, in general, a new generation, not in harmony with that severe architecture, populates the châteaux of the Berri, veritable stone nests from which the birds of prey have disappeared. Luxury, and even Parisian coquetry, often cheers up those feudal bastilles with ornaments not in harmony with the rudeness of the frame. Young women dressed in the manner of our great cities do the honors of their drawing rooms with a charming ease and grace, regarding which the formers chatelaines are mutely indignant in their old portraits, hung religiously on the walls.

A remarkable fact is that the destructions, however profound and relentless they have been, have not been able entirely to remove those ineradicable châteaux from the earth. Peasants have come after the demolishers to extract the ruins from the soil, but they have not succeeded. Those monuments to feudal history have remained intact in their foundations, to attest to the future the passage of a race of almost unknown giants. Herds of heavily-kneeling oxen, or a few light goats suspended in the indestructible remains of those venerable constructions finish forming for the traveler tableaux full of information and poetry.

When one studies the places, one does not take long to remark that the châteaux spared by the ravages of the Fronde that remain standing in the region are almost all constructions devoid of military importance, all the value of which depends on their position and the defense of their neighbors. When the primary supports of the feudal regime were demolished, the other châteaux were allowed to subsist, incapable of casting any shadow over royalty. Almost all the constructions of the Middle Ages still standing in the Berri, in fact, served castles now fallen as powerful auxiliaries that protected them from surprise attacks. It is thus that the Château de Chazelet, which remains intact, found in its allies de Luzeret and de Chassin-Grimont, brothers in arms who fortified it and which demolition attained for that reason. The feudal dwellings now overturned offer, in fact, remains of keeps, posterns, crenellated towers and all the luxury of fortifications of which other conserved castles are far from presenting the savage and menacing aspect. Among those monuments, as with men, it is the strongest that were the first to succumb.

The habitation of the Comte de B***, somber and severe as it seems in our day with its imposing mass of towers, its thick walls, its drawbridge, its battlements, its low doors, its interior courtyards surrounded by ditches and its firm and massive seating on the summit of a hill, would have been little more than a pleasure house for the rude barons of the Middle Ages.

IV

THE curiosity of the inhabitants then found itself divided between the solitary château and the habitation of a German physician who had come to take up residence in the locale a few months previously. The house he occupied, half a league from the château, was a former presbytery whose ruins he had had repaired. Sheltered to the north by a thick black forest, it received the full blast of the south-westerly winds; the dilapidated roofs, beaten then by stormy gusts, allowed the debris of mossy tiles to fall in rainy weather. An enclosure of brambles and living hedges surrounded a small garden in which a few legumes, fruit trees and vine-stocks vegetated. The pigeons of the château loved to come and repose on the roof of the house or drink familiarly from a spring of fresh water that emerged from the ground in the middle of the vegetable patch.

The owner of that abandoned house was named Georges Fritzs.

People were greatly astonished by his way of life. The hunters who went to catch swallows or kingfishers alongside ponds often found him, motionless and pensive, on the water's edge. At other times, he was seen plunging alone into the utmost depths of the woods, or fraying at random an adventurous route through the uncultivated heaths of which the Berri offers the sad and savage spectacle in places. He seemed to be fleeing the society of the local inhabitants as a matter of character, and they did not take long to spread malicious gossip regarding his grim humor and his bizarre behavior.

Although the bourgeois of the region did not often invite him to their tables, on the other hand, the stony paths bordered by living hedges that snaked mysteriously under the trees often saw him sitting in their shade with an open book in his lap.

Among the peasants, Georges Fritzs had another reputation; he passed for a sorcerer.

The truth is that, drawn by anxiety and the curiosity of mystery, he had engaged at a young age in the somber forest of occult sciences. *Faust* and the tales of Hoffmann had been his first favorite reading.[1]

His father, an old German alchemist who had died in an explosion, had initiated him subsequently into cabalistic secrets. No one

---

1 E. T. A. Hoffmann (1776-1822) was a favorite author of the French Romantics; one semi-documentary story in the 1877 collection employs him as a character, referring to him as "Théodore," an appellation also employed in a story by Jules Janin, which similarly employs him as a exemplary character. Janin was a close friend of Charles Nodier, two of whose stories feature a character named Théodore, an opium-eating bibliomaniac. The hallucinations featured in Théophile Gautier's story "Le Club des hachichins," mistaken by some readers and critics as non-fiction, are explicitly derived from works by Hoffmann.

was able to remonstrate with him regarding those tenebrous operation of magic, which always imply a certain grandeur, since limited human intelligence then required an infernal and uncanny power to push back the limits of the real.

Since then, he had made the acquaintance of a disciple of Mesmer, who served to guide him through the tenebrous labyrinth of the secrets of nature.

Georges Fritzs had studied medicine, but he did not believe in that curative art; he only had faith in the mysterious and beneficent principle that nature has put within us to soothe the woes of our brethren. His remedies were simple; they consisted of the power of the gaze, freemasonic signs and a generous breath of his lips communicated to glasses full of water. The good doctor only asked of his patients a little faith. "Believe," he said, "and you will be cured."

The poor peasants soon abandoned the other physicians of the region and hastened to follow Monsieur Fritzs. The others fell into a great jealousy; they denounced their rival to the curé, who referred the matter to the bishop. It caused a great stir in an ignorant country where the *Petit Albert* still reigned in all its potency.[1] The local clergy took sides against him, and if the young doctor had been living in the sixteenth century he would doubtless have been legally burned as a magician.

Georges Fritzs was simply a magnetizer.

---

1 *Secrets merveilleux de la magie naturelle et cabalistique du Petit Albert* was one of several fake "grimoires" first published in the early eighteenth-century—actually an anthology of second-hand materials of highly dubious authenticity, whose title coupled it with another grimoire falsely attributed to the thirteenth-century Dominican scholar known as Albertus Magnus—which took advantage of a wave of fashionability that boosted numerous illicit publications to great popularity when Louis XV's censors lost control of printing in France. It was the best-seller of its curious genre, and was still found secreted in many poor homes in the early twentieth century.

V

THE former presbytery near the château in which he lived, as we have said, was an old construction appended to a ruined church; a vast and cold ground floor, the ceiling of which was striped by huge beams, received daylight through two large windows overlooking a small courtyard where a few chickens clucked; a wooden stairway had its base in that room and led at a rather stiff slope to two rooms, one of which was Georges' bedroom and the other that of his domestic; a few old armchairs, a table and an old clock hanging on the wall formed the entire furniture. Externally, the little house did not lack character; a vine threw its foliage above the door, and a few stones detached from the walls had been replaced by pieces of Gothic sculpture taken from the ruins of the church.

Georges Fritzs had also built a small pavilion with that curious debris at the bottom of his garden, which served him as a retreat; it was there that he devoted himself to tenebrous experiments in occult science.[1] He spent long hours in there and emerged therefrom with his face pale, his eyes haggard and his voice hoarse, without anyone being able to discover the nature of his work or his anxieties. All that could be seen was smoke fuming over the roof during his alchemical operations from the mouth of a high chimney.

One day he was devoting himself to an endeavor of the Great Work when his aged maidservant came to knock rudely at the door, contrary to all instructions. Fritzs opened it. A white vapor was emerging from a crucible warmed to red heat by a gas fire and spread

1 The fact that there is no further reference to Georges' alchemical experiments in the latter chapters of the story adds plausibility to the notion that they might have been written belatedly, in a different epoch.

a suffocating obscurity throughout the room, which made Marthe cough several times.

"What's the matter with you?" Fritzs said to her, ill-humoredly.

Old Marthe explained to him then that there was a domestic in the courtyard clad in the livery of the château.

"Eh! What do I care?" said Georges, with a slight shrug of his shoulders.

He had carefully put a diamond-shaped lid over his crucible, which had only contained, thus far, a little ash.

Marthe returned mildly to the charge. She gave a lengthy account of the seigneur, Monsieur le Comte de B***, and then she added something that never fails in its effect on a young man: that it was said that there was a young woman, seventeen years old, at the château.

"Have the domestic go into the house," said Fritzs, a little more calmly. "I'll join him there."

The comte's domestic was introduced into the ground floor. While awaiting her master,

Marthe passed a duster over the large oak table several times, and if it had depended on her, that table would have changed into an elegant orange-wood sideboard—but, unlike Georges Fritzs, she was ignorant of the art of transmutation.

When Fritzs came in, the domestic of the château handed him a folded letter in his master's handwriting:

> *Monsieur le docteur,*
>
> *I am sending you my domestic and my horses. I beg you to have yourself conducted to the château without delay. We are waiting for you.*
>
> *Comte de B****

"I'm at your disposal," said Fritzs, after a pause.

The young doctor climbed into the comte's carriage, and when the domestic had closed the door, the coachman whipped his horses.

VI

THE carriage had been rolling for a quarter of an hour over a stony path when Georges Fritzs discovered the high towers of the château. In response to the coachman's voice the gate turned on rusty and lazy hinges, which seemed to have forgotten that exercise. An untidy first courtyard surrounded by low buildings, which doubtless served as barns, garages and stables, led via a drawbridge to a second interior courtyard, which was paved and neat. A great silence reigned over that second part of the château. A ditch full of water in which ducks dappled with plaques of bright metallic colors were floating, surrounded a cold and taciturn enclosure. Rare windows sunk into thick masonry and veiled internally by curtains maintained an air of mystery over the entire habitation. Pigeons and swifts crowned the summits of the towers with their mingled flight. A few dogs, of a generous breed once trained for hunting, now lay their bleak heads on the pavement, and seemed to be conforming to the general sadness that reigned throughout the vast edifice.

An aged manservant clad in black velvet, with a silver chain around his neck, saluted the young doctor silently and mounted before him a spiral staircase that opened to the courtyard by a low door framed by ancient stone ribs. Georges Fritzs followed him.

The stairway took them to a sumptuously decorated drawing room. The domestic moved an armchair and asked the young doctor to wait for Monsieur le Comte, who would come, and then withdrew. Left alone, Fritzs look round curiously. His gaze paused principally in the depths of the room on an oil painting bordered by a golden frame. It depicted a young woman of such great beauty that Georges decided to interpret the canvas as a work of the imagination and not for a portrait copied from nature.

After a delay of a few minutes, the door opened quietly and Monsieur le Comte de B*** came in. Pallor and despair were inscribed upon his grave and severe visage. He made a sign of his hand to the doctor bidding him to sit down beside him in an armchair.

"Monsieur," said the comte, "you are dealing with a man who has need of your discretion."

"I have never failed in that, Monsieur," said Fritzs.

"I believe you," said the comte, and fell back into silence.

"May I know, finally, what brings me here?" hazarded the impatient young doctor.

"This is it. I have a daughter . . ."

At that point, the old man's voice died away and his forehead darkened.

"Is she ill?" asked Fritzs, wanting to hasten the explanation.

"You have said it."

The old man made a gesture to indicate that the head was the seat of the malady.

"She's mad?" Georges divined.

"I wish to Heaven that she were," said the dejected old man. "Madness is at least a violent, and sometimes inspired, state that takes its victims beyond human limits. My daughter is less than that.

"The poor child is an idiot."

VII

THERE was a door-curtain in the drawing room in red damask, which doubtless masked a neighboring room, and which
was inflated from time to time by gusts of
compressed air.

Monsieur de B*** lifted a corner of that
curtain with his hand.

George then saw, outlined in the decorated door-frame, a resplendent beauty. She
was sitting nonchalantly in an armchair in the
middle of a room with windows open over the
garden, obscured by lowered blinds. She was
crumpling flowers and ribbons between her
fingers.

Fritzs was dazzled; the oil painting in the
drawing room had seemed impossible to him

at first; now it remained far inferior to the model.

The woman he had before his eyes was named Pulcherie. It was a name that suited her well.

A crown of seventeen white roses, symbolic of her years, which were only spring flowers for her, ornamented her forehead. She was a brunette. Two smooth tresses severely fitted over the temples framed her oval face; the rest of her hair was drawn back and knotted behind the head with a Greek simplicity. Her eyes were large and dark. Her chin was firm and the line of her nose, attached to the forehead without rupture, gave her profile an antique appearance of great character. If we descend from the face, which was a model of grace and severity, to the magnificence of the neck, shoulders, arms, hands and infinitely small feet, we encounter an ensemble of ravishing forms that we would not discover easily in other women.

The idea occurred to Georges Fritzs that Pulcherie had exhausted in beauty all the art of nature. The girl was an unfinished work. To make a soul as beautiful as the body, the Creator would perhaps have had to resume the endeavor for a second time.

The work of nature was borne entirely to the mortal envelope of the woman and had stopped there. It was the form with all its splendor and richness, but the spirit was lacking. There was in Pulcherie the first half of an accomplished woman, but the second was not there. She was, therefore, an imperfect creature into whom the last breath of life had not yet descended.

On coming into the world she had given rise to the most fortunate hopes. Such a child had never been seen. Everywhere there was an endless admiration and astonishment on her account. People could not get over her pretty arms, her tiny feet and her large eyes, and Madame de B*** found herself triply happy as a mother. But with the years, the age of reason having come, the child had remained.

Pulcherie scarcely had the intelligence of a three-year-old girl. Her lovely mouth only formed inarticulate sounds. She was neither mute nor deaf, but, having no thought, she could not make any use of language. More often than not she spent entire days in silence, dejected and nonchalant. Sunlight gave her a little life; she raised her head then like a flower, opened her dark slumberous eyes wide and gazed around her vaguely, with astonishment; then she fell back into an armchair, her dark eyes veiled by white eyelids, her head as heavy as a sleeping poppy, and she resumed her immobility.

The young doctor did not take long to remark in her the absence of the animation and movement that are the beauty of life. Her eyes were large and dark but devoid of gaze; her mouth, admirably made, had the insignificant and dainty smile of a child's mouth; her magnificent arms, her waist and her regal neck were not sustained by the will, allowing them to dangle or flex slackly; her entire body seemed obedient to the law of gravitation that attracts inanimate objects toward the earth.

It was evident that the beautiful body, in order to be perfect, required the help of a mind. A pretty woman who is intelligent is pretty a thousand times over, whereas Pulcherie only had one expression, doubtless charming but always the same. Only a soul, incessantly mobile in her thoughts and emotions, can operate that miracle of the multiplication of a woman, which responds to the infinite desires of our heart.

After a few moments of mute admiration, Georges Fritzs was astonished to find Pulcherie a little less beautiful than at first glance; he started then to look for a flaw, but he did not find any; she really was perfect in every respect, but there was always that same expression and that same monotonous beauty, while another woman, possessed of intelligence and heart, would have changed several times in his presence.

It is not enough for a body and a face to please; it also requires the physiognomy to be involved. Physiognomy is the style of the face, and as there is no style without thought, Pulcherie had none. She lacked the emphasis that makes full value of the beauty of a face, and which sometimes goes as far as effacing ugliness. The uniform character of her features ended up leading to ennui. Everything about her was well made and well proportioned; she only lacked a little soul in order to be completely beautiful.

VIII

THE comte went into a few details regarding the mental state of his daughter with the young doctor.

Pulcherie was a beautiful ignorant flower who was completely unaware of her beauty. It had, however, been remarked that she was not indifferent to all coquetry. That sentiment is so natural to a woman! She liked to look at herself in a mirror when she had lilacs in her hair, necklaces around her neck and bracelets on her wrists. But it was an insipid and colorless joy that quit her very rapidly. Around her, people, nature and art said absolutely nothing to her; for all of that she only had one facial expression and one gaze. Her mother imagined that she was recognized by her, but deep down, she loved Zizime, the household dog, just as much.

A great inequality of humor made her pass without reason from laughter to tears. Those vague sorrows and joys followed unknown instincts. It was possible that her nature, incomplete and crude as it was, had its laws, but the notion of them escaped even scholars. As a great naturalist has said about monsters, following Montaigne, it is probable that idiots and madmen do not exist for God.

Pulcherie only had the life that flowers have: beauty and tears. At times she had the gaiety of a bird that sings without being aware of it, and at other times the dolor of a sensitive plant that withdraws its petals when fearful or afflicted. Was Pulcherie happy in her condition? No one knew. It was probable that she was hardly aware of being alive.

During the time that Fritzs had been studying her, Pulcherie had only made one sole movement. Her distracted hand had searched behind her head for the tortoiseshell comb that maintained her hair in a forceful and magnificent knot. A black snake then rolled over her shoulders and her white dress. She started to play with her loose hair, scattering it around her like a veil.

Fritzs advanced toward her and took Pulcherie's hands in his. She let him do it. No blush or any of the unequivocal signs that always betray, even in an alienated young woman, the modesty of her sex at the sight of a young man, was manifest in her extinct face. Georges blew on his subject's forehead; several times his fingers wandered over her arms, shoulders and bosom at a distance, in order to expel the fluid therefrom. A slight quiver of the heart, at the sight of all those magnificent forms, caused the young doctor's hand to tremble from time to time.

Magnetism has its sacramental aspect, which consists of passes, gazes and warm and penetrating breaths; those signs are the conductors of the will and serve to *establish a rapport*. Although the phenomena of the science enter for the most part into a very elevated sphere of intelligence, they are nevertheless submissive to a positive and absolutely material mechanism that puts the soul in train of action. Georges Fritzs was dealing, in his first session, with an instrument so coarse and so disordered that he could not extract anything satisfactory therefrom; one might have thought that a great musician—Monsieur Liszt, for example—was playing *against* a piano, all of whose keys were mute or out of tune; there was no possible scale. He tried to put some accord between those disorganized keys, but without success. All that he was able to observe was that Pulcherie, magnetized after a fashion by his action, inclined her body slightly toward his. Magnetism, thus reduced to a simple material force, scarcely surpasses the laws of attraction in the physical world.

Fritzs could not help thinking that there were many women who would sacrifice anything in the world to have that beauty, which would serve them admirably for the happiness of the men that they loved. He wondered at the same time what reasons God had had for refusing to give it to them, in order to give it to this poor futile and vain creature who could not make any usage of it. That gave him grounds to hope that Providence might come to the aid of nature.

Pulcherie's cure presented itself surrounded by obstacles; it was almost temerity to attempt a cure in which the most skillful, including Monsieur Esquirol himself,[1] had all failed, but Georges Fritzs had faith in the magic of his science, and that faith sustained him above difficulties, as Saint Peter was once sustained above the waves.

---

1 The alienist Jean-Étienne-Dominique Esquirol (1772-1840) established his initial reputation working of the Salpêtrière and also had his own private asylum. He was the first physician to offer a public lecture course on mental illnesses and he pioneered the reform of the clinical asylums of Paris that shifted the treatment of madness entirely into a curative medical context; he played a leading role in the incorporation of the asylums of France into an institutional structure formalized by law in 1838.

The young doctor looked into the hand of Pulcherie, for he put a little chiromancy into his art; its lines were pale and effaced, like printed characters spoiled in the run, which marked a great sign of imbecility; the hand is the satellite of the head and the book of the intelligence.

"Well?" asked Monsieur de B***, at the end of the session, "do you have any hope of an effect?"

"I shall continue," said Fritzs.

"When will you come back, Doctor?"

"Tomorrow, Monsieur le Comte."

Fritzs bowed and left.

He did not sleep that night. Pulcherie was as beautiful and as cold as a Galatea of marble. He thought about means of communicating life to her, but by dint of thinking about it, of passing that young head of alabaster whiteness before the eyes of his soul, he had the fate of Pygmalion and fell in love with his statue.

But who is the amorous individual who does not sculpt the ideal, like Pygmalion?

IX

GEORGES FRITZS had a nature apart. Blond with blue eyes, he embodied the German mysticism that incessantly bears its gaze toward the heavens. His body was frail and delicate; life seemed to have withdrawn in him to the superior regions of the head, which were vast and well-developed in him. The Bible doubtless intended to designate those extraordinary forms of the cranium when it represents to us in several places God manifesting himself to men on high mountains.

Since his visit to the château he seemed even dreamier and more contemplative than ever. Plunged mysteriously for entire days in the depths of the woods, without taking any nourishment, he seemed, like all unquiet minds tormented by tenebrous discoveries, to feel a need to get closer to nature.

Sometimes that infinite anxiety burst forth in somber and lyrical deliria, which endorsed the local rumors regarding the relations of Georges Fritzs and spirits, species of beings very unfamiliar to Berrichons, who are mostly heavy and dull beings who tend to justify the proverb. He was often seen passing over high mountains, his hair in the wind, his agitated mouth murmuring a few vague words, his eyes fixed on the horizon, whose boundless extent he devoured with a grim gaze. The old maidservant Marthe began to enter into her master's great torment and to fear that a chariot of fire might descend one day from Heaven to carry him off like the prophet Elijah.

Georges Fritzs was researching life. Like the ancient alchemists who demanded generative breath from nature in order to animate statues or automata of their invention, the young doctor demanded from the stars, from light, from the winds and the waters, a soul for Pulcherie, who was, in effect, scarcely more than an automaton of flesh and a warm statue.

He wanted to inhale momentarily the fecund and intelligent breath that incessantly populates creatures without number in the heavens and on earth. Inclining his mouth over the abyss, he sought to draw into his insatiable lungs the primitive element of life; but the human breast cannot contain that creative breath, and the ungraspable soul fled the avid lips of the scholar incessantly.

Georges Fritzs had days of despair and dejection during which he appealed to death, but soon the eternal concert of creation invited him again to the inexhaustible joys of the infinite being. Often, in his dementia, the young doctor, who believed in the transmission of souls, applied his lips to the dying mouths of young women. He demanded that their extinct organization surrender to him its principle of life, in order to animate the incomplete and unintelligent Eve, only partly emerged from the eternal womb of nature.

In brief, plunged into all the anguish and melancholy of a mental childbirth, Georges Fritzs floated there, as somber, indecisive and immense as the creative spirit over the face of the waters.

X

FUNDAMENTAL to human amour is a great desire for creation. Georges Fritzs became passionately attached to Pulcherie, like a poet to a work he is meditating or a sculptor to the block of marble from which he wants to draw life.

It was not the incomplete and dubious creature that the doctor was pursuing with an infinite desire, but the ideal of that semi-realized woman that he wanted to attain in the mysterious depths of divine prescience, in order to force her to emerge from the void where she remained as if enveloped. Pulcherie's intelligence resembled those beautiful images of Daphne partly engaged in an opaque and invasive bark that retains her in captivity; it was necessary to break those bonds and take that immobile soul, whose eyes had not yet seen the light, out of her prison.[1]

There was a woman in Pulcherie, as there is a statue in a formless block of marble, but it was necessary to disengage her. Georges Fritzs made himself the artist of that mysterious creation.

The first trials were long and laborious. The robust organization of Mademoiselle de B*** opposed a despairing insensibility to Georges Fritzs' efforts. The reiterated signs and energetic breathing that ordinarily bring disturbance or slumber to torpid limbs, and the fixed gazes posed directly upon the vague and drowned eyes of a subject, encountered nothing in that inanimate young woman but the stupid inertia of matter. He might as well have been trying to magnetize a milestone. The young doctor began to lose patience and

1 The story of the nymph Daphne, changed into a laurel tree by Apollo after rejecting his advances, as featured in Ovid's *Metamorphoses* and elsewhere, became a popular subject in Renaissance art.

to renounce the chimera so much caressed of creating in that imperfect being a woman in her image.

That struggle between Georges' creative jet and the recalcitrant, inert, lumpen subject on which its action was exercised offered in miniature an image of God struggling with the formless mass of the brute and primitive world in order to extract the first manifestations of life therefrom. However, by dint of perseverance and toil, of brooding, in a way, a future formation within that mental chaos in which cold and diffuse elements were agitating pellmell, Fritzs obtained a few exterior signs that permitted him to hope that those incoherent and disordered signs resembled the first monstrous phenomena that nascent nature developed without regulation in the world. Science informs us, in fact, that the globe we inhabit passed through a long infancy before arriving, via a series of experiments and ameliorations, at the solid and adult state in which humans found it at their advent.

Georges Fritzs, encouraged by those first fugitive shadows, doubtless of a life still latent and vague, the laws of which it was impossible to grasp, continued his initial trials with more ardor than ever. With the torch of intelligence in hand, he sought to penetrate into the tenebrous depths of that imperfect and bleak creature surrounded by a void, from which nothing emerged except by means of a sort of internal vegetation common to plants and zoophytes.

XI

GEORGES FRITZS exercised all the influences of magnetism on Pulcherie.

We are entering here into a fantastic world in which plausibility no longer has any meaning, in which all the ordinary and anticipated rules are abruptly inverted, in which the pilot traveling therein has only one possible compass, faith.

The reader must therefore be kind enough to believe us when we talk about that tenebrous world, in which human reason advances blindly through a series of occult phenomena, of which he cannot follow the thread or penetrate the cause. The ordinary laws of nature, suddenly inverted by unknown agents, seem casually to disconcert the efforts of our limited intelligence, which struggles in vain in the icy regions of doubt.

In the beginning, Pulcherie had seen Georges Fritzs without repugnance; on the contrary, she felt attracted to him by a vague instinct; but since the young doctor, by means of signs and the disturbing effects of his will, had brought trouble into his subject's torpid limbs, the latter struggled against that influence, uttering fearful cries and writhing, pushing away the magnetic influence with her hands. There was between them something like the sublime struggle that the Gospel so often sets before our eyes when it shows us Jesus Christ taming a foaming and rebellious demon in the body of a possessed individual, which resists him: "Son of God, why are you tormenting me?"

That resistance of Pulcherie to the omnipotent action of Georges must have resembled even more closely the discontentment of chaos when the creative energy forced it to emerge reluctantly from is long primitive repose, to put it into movement and labor toward the formations of life. The faculties of the imperfect being, asleep in her idle senses, resented the foreign force that drew them toward development and action; they were complaisant in their oblivion.

In spite of the rebellions of the formless nature that refused life. Georges ended up by taming and subjugating it. Intelligent force prevailed over the resistance of blind nature; mind vanquished the flesh. Master of the movements and functions of his subject, Georges Fritzs acquired over her an empire limited to the organism but already omnipotent. The mysterious influences of the magnetizer in this respect are familiar; Fritzs introduced his will into Pulcherie's senses, in such a way as to extract the most extraordinary actions therefrom. The subject was no longer, externally, anything but a docile harp on the strings over which Georges Fritzs' sovereign fingers played, in order to produce all the chords he desired.

Often, he took pleasure in drawing Pulcherie's hand into his own, where it remained fixed, in a way. At other times, Mademoiselle de B*** repeated all Fritzs' movements like a submissive shadow fatally drawn by another body, the fugitive oscillations of which it follows in space. But those influences, so marvelously attained, were still only superficial; fundamentally, Pulcherie still remained the same; her poor, cold, bleak and crippled intelligence remained no less immobile and impenetrable in the depths of the tenebrous prison of the senses, into which Georges' genius had yet to break.

Pulcherie's treatment strongly resembled the abduction of Eurydice, which a Latin poet recounts in such beautiful verses. It was a matter, in order to liberate that captive soul and bringing her back into the light, of penetrating into the profound Tartarus of a dense and tenebrous nature in which hardly anything floated but the vague and confused shadows of thought. It was necessary to traverse a motionless and heavy night populated by formless chimeras; the black solitudes that surrounded in Pulcherie's head the imprisoned and dead intelligence resembled the obscure forests of an eternal horror, the miry marshes of the Cocytus and the cold limits of the inexorable Styx, thrice folded back upon itself. At the entrance, like Cerberus with the three gaping maws, the physical force of that recalcitrant nature was on guard. In spite of the dubious success of his enterprise, Georges, sustained like Orpheus by the mysterious harmonies of an invisible lyre and driven by amour, entered into the obscure realms in which his Eurydice was languishing.

XII

A MAGNETIZER does not always act directly upon his subject; he often makes use of intermediaries to which he confides his power. The insensible objects that he is able to subjugate then guard and transmit his will like faithful servants.

One evening, Georges Fritzs was seen trying making signs to one of the trees in the park of the château; the servants of the house laughed at him, not knowing what the man was doing with that tree. The following day, when she awoke in the morning, Pulcherie testified by gestures an intention to go out; her women could not prevent her from so doing. Ordinarily, Mademoiselle de B*** never left her room, retained as she was by a dull idleness. She was lent an arm to descend the steps of the perron that gave access to the garden. The park outlined its curtains of foliage in the depths of the garden, where impetuous gusts of wind were making large rents here and there.

As soon as she set foot in the avenue of the park, Pulcherie quit the arm of her maidservant and marched by herself, as if drawn by an inevitable force, toward the tree that Fritzs had magnetized the day before; it was a holly bristling with foliage. She lay down in the shadow of the tree and went to sleep there. The leaves, moist with dew and disturbed by the wind, seemed to be shaking over the forehead of the beautiful sleeper, one by one, all of Fritzs' thoughts; then a few unintelligible words, like those one attempts in a dream, formed partially and died on her parted lips.

She slept in the wood until nightfall. Her father, alarmed, tried to extract her from that slumber, but he was unable to succeed. Her arm was moved violently, and a golden pin was even plunged into her bare shoulder, but she gave no sign of life. Finally, George Fritzs having arrived, he extended his hand to her and said: "It's me, Pulcherie; get up."

And she woke up.

From then on, Mademoiselle de B*** came every day to sleep for a few hours in that place; she was never mistaken with regard to the tree; the magnetized holly, even though it was in the utmost depths of the wood, was recognizable for her among all the other holly trees and it attracted her forcefully to its shade. A heavy blindfold, steeped in forgetfulness and slumber, immediately fell over her eyes and she fell asleep. That tree had a beneficent repose for her, mingled with dreams and visions, which created hope in this dictum of Fritzs': Pulcherie's soul could only wake up in slumber.

In the same park there was another enchanted tree; it was a bushy walnut that Georges Fritzs often magnetized. That one had the effect of repelling Pulcherie and casting into her head a contrary and an iniquitous fluid. She often tried to approach it in spite of that, but the resistance on the tree's part increased in drastic proportion. Pulcherie felt violently driven back to a great distance. She sometimes tried, in vain, to struggle against that repulsive and distressing current but it was always necessary to yield. That tree, which defended itself victoriously against any approach, would have awakened in anyone but Pulcherie a surprise mingled with terror.

There was still nothing in all that to awaken anything in her above the laws of matter. Similar rapports exist in all brute substances that attract or repel one another. Almost all the phenomena observed thus far in Pulcherie, therefore, entered more or less into the effects of positive and negative electricity.

XIII

SUCH frequent and singular experiments could not fail, at length, to resound in the soul and agitate it in its torpor. That soul still refused to appear; carefully enveloped in the tenebrous depths of obtuse and blind senses, it opposed a bleak resistance to the light suddenly brought all around it; like certain birds hostile to daylight, it plunged solitarily into its night.

Georges Fritzs tried harder than ever to pursue it there and force it out.

We shall not follow in detail all the progress of that mental battle, the gradual and fugitive nuances of which could not fail to fatigue the reader. It will be sufficient for us to say that every day brought appreciable signs of development. Pulcherie's head was at work.

For some time, during these magnetic sessions, Mademoiselle de B*** had been agitating her lips as if to break her eternal bleak idiotic silence, but sound was lacking to her moving lips; certain invisible bonds seemed to retain slavish speech on the edge of her impotent mouth. She suffered ostentatiously from that invincible mutism, which held her in a dismal and inert vegetal state. In vain Fritzs tried to aid his subject's efforts and to extract speech violently from her rebellious lips; he could not do it; the organs, jealous of seeing the soul escape their enslavement, seems to want to retain it in the extreme limits of its prison. It agitated indignantly in order to vanquish that well-guarded passage, but in vain; after futile efforts, it fell back into an incurable languor that drove Fritzs to despair.

If we relate once more our thought regarding the birth of the world to the mental birth of Pulcherie we seem to perceive secret and mysterious analogies; we willingly imagine a moment when, animate creatures having not yet appeared on earth, there must have been a great and lamentable silence there. Everything was quiet. Universal intelligence, which lives everywhere and prior to everything, existed; speech, or the Word, similarly existed with it, but, retained by the inert and indocile bonds of brute matter, speech could not be liberated. A slave, and latent, so to speak, it required, in order to emerge, more relaxed organs to lend it their collaboration; fatally enveloped in the mute ligaments of a plant or a mineral, it aspired to the mouth of superior animals in order to take flight and form.

The first voice that made itself heard in the world was an immense event impossible to describe; that voice was the mysterious sign of the deliverance of the spirit, retained thus far by crude bonds in the base and tenebrous regions of matter.

XIV

FRITZS dreamed increasingly every day of the mental birth of Pulcherie to a more extensive life. Like the Jehovah of the Bible, he agitated the formless elements of his creation in order to disengage the ideal that he had in his soul. For her part, Pulcherie seemed increasingly ill with intelligence; a decisive manifestation was generally expected at the château.

One evening, when Mademoiselle de B*** was in the drawing room sitting on a divan, Georges took her hand and said: "Sleep!"

She went to sleep immediately, for Georges, by means of exercise, had conquered a limitless empire over her. She remained plunged in the silence of heavy slumber for a few minutes; but Fritzs, fatigued by the mute state that would soon have lasted for a month, resolved abruptly to put an end to it. With that intention, he presented an iron rod before her stomach.

Such wands, of which magicians made use in their evocations, and to which superstitious ages attributed so many marvels, have the principal effect of forcing speech from the rebellious lips of a somnambulist.

The vast and somber drawing room was only illuminated by a large lamp in the form of a crystal globe, which shed a transparent light on the magical scene. Monsieur de B*** and his wife remained silent. As soon as the tip of the wand encountered Pulcherie's breast the young woman stood up with a supple and smooth movement, took a few steps toward the mantelpiece, placed herself in contemplation before the mirror, placed a wild flower in her hair, and cried in a low voice, admiring herself: "Beautiful!"

That was the first cry and the first revelation of the woman: "I'm beautiful!" A cloud fell from Pulcherie's eyes.

Previously, that mute and insensible creature had resembled the world that we inhabited before the advent of the first human. She was beautiful, like virgin and primitive nature, but devoid of knowledge and at a pure loss; thought lacked form, the spectator a spectacle. Intelligence and sentiment entered into that woman of their own accord; a human soul appeared on the brute earth of her own beauty. Those large eyes, thus far distracted and vague, that pretty mouth condemned to silence, those nonchalant and idle white hands, all those previously incoherent marvels, scattered and floating, so to speak, here and there, arrived at being knotted together and becoming comprehensible in Pulcherie's head, just as the entire universe became understood, and admired itself in the first human.

"I'm beautiful!" That was the first cry of triumph of that women escaped from the shadows of the void, who contemplated herself with astonishment; she was Eve emerging from the flank of the man, parading her dazzled gaze around her and then, touching her long loose hair, remarking her unfamiliar arms, her royally white hands, her magnificent alabaster shoulders, smiled at seeing herself thus made. That smile blossoming on the ravishing visage of Pulcherie was a ray of sublime light that illuminated the entire drawing room.

Georges Fritzs, fearing that a longer vision might fatigue Pulcherie's nascent faculties, left her, astonished and calm, in the arms of her father, who witnessed the birth of his child, in a sense, for the second time.

XV

THE young doctor scarcely contained in his slender breast the outbursts of an insensate joy and pride, which did not take long to fall before new obstacles.

Magnetism is a fabulous world in which the success that one believes that one has conquered entirely often escapes you in unexpected directions. Fritzs had certainly stirred that idle intelligence; he had been to seek it in its darkness in order to drag it by the hair, like the ancient pythoness, toward the light of thought, but, in addition to the fact that it did not take long to fall back into the torpor of its silence, the young scientist realized that he had done nothing thus far to penetrate as far as the heart of the woman.

The spirit of women is in the heart rather than the head.

Pulcherie's intelligence had certainly pierced the thick cloud that enveloped her with darkness momentarily, but that pale sun devoid of warmth soon reentered into darkness; it was necessary to search elsewhere for a warmer and more durable light. After the magnetic action, Pulcherie, although lacking discernment and real affection, manifested a few of the blind penchants that attract animals toward their fellows or drive them away. Such secret affinities exist even among inanimate beings like plants as minerals. Georges Fritzs counted on transforming, over time, those gross instincts into more tender and delicate sentiments.

In search of Pulcherie's heart for several days, Fritzs surrounded his subject with the most tender cares. Having faith in the agent that a man can transmit by his will to inanimate objects, and which the same objects then communicate to the persons who touch them, he had recourse to all the sortileges of sentiment. Magnetism furnished him with a thousand means of maintaining an intimate and mysterious commerce with Pulcherie; often, for example, he made her drink a glass of water that he had taken care to charge with fluid by means of his breath, which was, in a sense, giving her his soul to drink. Pulcherie, surrounded by Georges with a kind of amorous atmosphere, rediscovered him in everything she touched, for he had been careful to act upon all the objects in the room. Flowers, the bagatelles of her toilette, and even the nourishment that she took, were like sacraments under which the constant thought of the young doctor hid.

Magnetism might well be one of the sensible forms of amour.

We have already mentioned the holly tree under which Georges' magnetic action put Pulcherie to sleep. Trees play an important role in the annals of mesmeric science. The just celebrity that was attached in the last century to the centenarian elm of Buzancy[1] is well known; in its shade Monsieur le Marquis de Puységur observed the first of the marvels of somnambulism.

For several weeks Georges Fritzs had been exercising his magnetic power on one of the apple trees in the garden. Because of that, the apple tree in question was known to the people of the château by the name of "the tree of knowledge."

One day in autumn, when Georges Fritzs was walking in the paths of the garden, doubtless thinking, like all magnetizers, about the

---

1 The original text has "Buzanel," but that must be a misprint; Buzancy was the name of the estate where Amand-Marie-Joseph de Chastenet, Marquis de Puységur (17651-1825) carried out many of his experiments. Puységur was one of the most significant popularizers of Mesmer's "magnetism," and his studies paved the way for its medical development in clinical asylums. The contributions he made to the theory of the unconscious mind were unappreciated at the time but were important precursors of developments made in the latter half of the nineteenth century.

universal soul. Mademoiselle de B*** gently pushed him by the arm toward the apple tree, which was laden with fruits. Was it a pure impulse of greed, or had Pulcherie seen in those apples, beautiful and delectable to the eye, what Georges Fritzs alone had put into them? Our young doctor had attempted to attach to those fruits a revelation of good and evil. Thus far, in fact, the consciousness of the beautiful idiot had been confused and surrounded by darkness.

Pulcherie extended her hand toward one of the branches laden with fruits; the branch was lowered gently, and she picked an apple, which she ate. Then the blindfold that covered in her the light of the mental senses was apparently removed; for, having seen her cleavage for the first time, which was naked before a young man, she blushed and made a scarf with her beautiful hands in order to hide it.

Mademoiselle de B*** then ran back to the château, utterly confused, casting off the garlands of flowers that were around her neck. She appeared to dread and fear the tree of knowledge thereafter, as if she had lost her innocent tranquility. It was in the shadow of the apple tree that she had discovered modesty, and perhaps also the attraction of forbidden fruit.

XVI

FRITZS came to the château as usual one evening and put Pulcherie to sleep by blowing on her forehead.

It was a beautiful evening in June. The windows of the drawing room, all wide open, allowed an intense perfume of thyme and flowering sainfoin to enter in gusts. An acrid breeze, which was beginning to be softened and moistened by dew, agitated the curtains from time to time or inflated them like sails. There were sounds of foliage in the air, stifled sighs and the songs of drowsy birds. One might have thought, judging by the religious character of the entire scene, that nature was singing her evening hymn. Monsieur and Madame de B*** could not escape the grave and solemn influence of the sky, still devoid of stars, in which the moon was rising, as pure, transparent and chaste as a young bride. Pulcherie was dressed in white, the color that suited her best. For some time she had begun to take care of her toilette herself; she had acquired a taste for dressing her hair, adjusting the pleats of her dress and putting flowers in her belt.

Mademoiselle de B*** seemed completely suspended on Fritzs' gaze. A new mystery passed between them in the midst of the mild mystery of nature in ecstasy; Fritzs' eyes shone like two stars. Suddenly, she took Georges' hands in hers and gazed at him with wide, staring eyes that did not see, and she said to him in a slow, profound, reflective voice that seemed to be savoring every letter of the words:

"Georges, I love you."

At the same moment she tipped her head back on the armchair; her long black hair was undone and the movement of her pulse had lost its rhythm; her heart had almost ceased beating. Magnetizers give that state the name of ecstasy. It succeeds somnambulism, and is ordinarily manifest after a vivid emotion. At that moment, the soul breaks its bonds and flies into a world from which it often does not return.

That eternal and divine phrase, *I love you*, had sent the young woman to heaven.

Ecstasy is a dangerous state, which the magnetizer can no longer govern and in which he ceases to be the master. His subject resists him, like anyone else. George Fritzs commanded Mademoiselle B*** to come back and give him a sign of life, but in vain; she took no account of it. On the contrary; she seemed to engage increasingly, as if with pleasure, with an unknown world very far from ours. The veins could no longer be seen beating in her discolored temples.

The entire household was in great anxiety. Fritzs' orders, which had previously encountered in Mademoiselle de B*** an ever-submissive slave, this time went as far as threats and violence without obtaining any result; a cadaver could not have opposed more insensibility. Fritzs was commencing to fall into exhaustion himself, and to believe, like everyone else present, that Pulcherie was dead. He gathered all his strength in order to command his subject one last time to wake up, but in spite of all the vehemence he put into it, the leaden slumber continued.

George Fritzs was inclining his head in impotent discouragement when, his lips having encountered the white and delicate hand of Mademoiselle de B***, he kissed it gently, like that of a young dead woman who is about to be buried.

Immediately, Pulcherie woke up.

"Georges," she said, opening her large eyes, still heavy with sleep and raising her hands to them, "why have you woken me up? I was so happy!"

The doctor left the château feeling taller than usual; it seemed to him that his head was touching the sky; it would not have taken much for him to believe that he had the gift of commanding all of nature. Having encountered in his path a flooded stream that blocked his passage, the desire took him, rather than going upstream to the wooden bridge, to walk on the water.

XVII

ONE final obstacle remained to vanquish, one last barrier to cross; it was necessary to transport into the waking state the progress that Pulcherie was developing every day in slumber, for thus far, her life had been little more than a dream, a shadow of that of Georges Fritzs.

The young doctor understood the difficulty; in seeking to overcome it seriously, he believed he had found a means in absence. The perpetual action that he was exercising on his subject had ended up retaining Mademoiselle B*** in a blind dependency that prevented her from growing freely. The young doctor therefore stayed away from the château for a few days; he addressed sleep to Pulcherie in a letter, which he had made by means of his will into a powerful narcotic; she went to sleep on touching the paper imbibed, so to speak, with slumber, and awoke of her own accord at the hour marked by Fritzs.

Magnetism is like the antique Chimera; while having rapid wings of which it makes use for flying, it nevertheless has feet that it often poses on the ground; its most surprising mental phenomena are disengaged by means of signs, conductors and talismans that are strongly reminiscent of the charms so common in the Middle Ages.

In Georges' absence, Pulcherie naturally began to think for herself.

From that moment on, Mademoiselle de B***'s condition improved from day to day. The poor mentally blind woman felt the scales falling from the eyes of her soul. For the first time she saw nature, the sky and beauty—for it is necessary to say that Pulcherie had previously known nothing of those marvels; to see and to hear something more is required than eyes and ears.

She was soon able to speak all the words of the language, for ideas naturally summon words. She recognized her father, her mother and the servants of the household. She learned to read and to pray. The immensity of creation and the spectacle of life gave her the sentiment of God.

Pulcherie repeated in herself the history of the first woman, who, if it is necessary to believe scholars, initially dragged out a vestal existence in plants, fixed to the soil, until, raising herself up with creation toward more perfect forms, she finally appeared in the world with a heart and a soul. It was then that she began to contemplate her surroundings, to comprehend and to love.

In effect, Pulcherie had at first led the life of flowers, had not even lived, but vegetated; to see her always immobile, barely inclined with a slight movement of the head, one might have taken her then for an idle young rose, neither thinking not toiling, whose purpose was to be beautiful. Now the flower had become a woman, doubtless gradually and with difficulty; it was the work of six days, but it had taken six months.

XVIII

MADEMOISELLE DE B*** profited a great deal, even physically, from Georges' treatment; her neck, previously negligent and idle, began to carry the head; her stature straightened; her eyes, previously devoid of a gaze, now emitted a fire that went to the soul. Pulcherie was definitely wholly beautiful. Her expression, once bleak and always similar, was now multiplied in a thousand various and charming fashions, as if by a miracle. Thought had come to poeticize and complete the form by animating it. There were no longer the cold and immobile lines of which nothing deranged the monotonous regularity; there was no longer the distracted and astonished attitude that was wearying to see. Pulcherie's visage now ran through all the notes of the infinite scale that is called sentiment.

Something suave and ineffable, that one can scarcely imagine in angels, distinguished that creature full of grace, who had, so to speak, not come to life by the ordinary means.

As soon as her speech was able to rid itself, during the waking state, of the last bonds that kept it captive, Pulcherie asked for Georges. On returning to the château, the young doctor commenced the education of his pupil.

That education was prompt and facile. In a way, Pulcherie divined Fritzs;' science; he was her book and she learned it by heart. Georges taught Pulcherie the names of flowers, birds and stars; he thus recounted all of creation to her. She listened like a new creature, who had emerged, ignorant and curious, from the shadows of the void,

Master and pupil delighted in adventurous walks through the fields; often, they both remained absorbed in vast spectacles; the great melancholy of silence and solitude filled their souls with a religious sadness. Taking from the woods their reverie, from the springs their eternal lament, from the horizons their immensity and from nature its infinite aspiration toward the heavens, they lived together in the whole universe.

The nature of the Berri, uncultivated and half wild, offers some resemblance to that of the primitive world, which we are wrong to represent as a terrestrial paradise and a delightful garden, whereas it was doubtless a brutal nature still enveloped in the darkness and asperities of infancy. A singular relationship existed between Pulcherie and the region where she lived; both offered the spectacle of a virgin creation gradually emerging from repose and the savage state. Around the young chatelaine the land of Berri was developing the signs of a nascent culture; industry was agitating in that chaos the elements of a rural prosperity, which tends to increase every day. Laborious streams, and even the indolent ones, were beginning to lend their waves to mills, forges and factories. The regular hammering of machinery filled the air with a monotonous sound that imitated the slow and heavy tread of civilization. United, in a way, with that nature on the path of progress and labor, Pulcherie developed with it.

Pulcherie's entirely new sensations were full of admiration and surprise; she was astonished by day and night, by stars and the sun, by the mute plant and the loquacious bird; all creation plunged her into infinite meditations. Georges' voice explained the causes of natural phenomena to her and opened her intelligence further and further to divine things.

He combined with the great book of nature other works of German and French poets, which she did not take long to read and comprehend. Fritzs interpreted the obscure passages for her, not without blushing when, by chance, there was mention therein of amour.

As Georges was a musician, he gave Pulcherie's voice, a poor warbler captive in her obscure throat, the key to the fields; the beautiful prisoner then began to sing accurately and with a perfect grace.

The education of Maemoiselle de B*** closely resembled a revelation; she divined in Georges the reason of things; she only learned from his mouth and read in his thought. Thus, she made rapid progress via the master's lessons, which were communicated to her in their entirety.

XIX

THAT perpetual relationship of the mind formed between Georges and Pulcherie a limitless sympathy. The word love, magical as it is, remains impotent to express that mysterious union, of which nature offers us no examples.

On days when one of them was sad, the other was too. When Georges suffered, Pulcherie suffered. If Fritzs blushed, a light pink cloud formed simultaneously on his friend's cheeks. In moments of gaiety, the same smile glided over their lips. At the piano, in the evening, the pupil could only sing with her master; they performed ravishing duets together; their voices sought one another with a perfect accord and followed the same movements, like two doves in flight in a completely calm sky.

The sight of nature affected both of them with similar emotions; they both had a similar gaze for the things of the earth and those of the sky; when one felt religiously moved the other prayed. They were the same being, thinking and loving twice in a single thought and a single amour. The affection that united them with one another was almost egotism.

Georges and Pulcherie did not even need words to communicate their thoughts; a sort of eloquent and energetic silence presided over their conversations. What one said, the other had already divined. They spent entire hours in those mysterious colloquia, during which their united hearts entered into society with the great family of creation.

The same instincts attracted them toward people and things or distanced them; people who displeased Fritzs could be certain of being disagreeable to Pulcherie, and reciprocally. The two of them had but one heart and one soul. Pulcherie found in Georges a sort of ideal self; she remembered in him, so to speak, everything that she ought to know.

They had analogous tastes in art, as in everything else; they were both attracted toward similar reading and it often happened to them to express the same idea, in almost the same words, without having communicated them in advance. Wanting to express that perfect conformity, Georges called Pulcherie his sister, and she called him her brother.

XX

MAGNETISM tightened the bonds of that union even more from day to day.

Fritzs exercised over Pulcherie the incredible power of the magnetizer, which consists of changing for his subject all natural relationships. The taste of fruits and the odor of flowers are submissive to his will; it is only the weight of bodies of which he cannot derange the sovereign laws at his whim. He can give roses the perfume of violets and peaches the taste of walnuts, as he can communicate to a light glove of Scottish thread the weight of an iron gauntlet. All of that retained the young woman in a fantastic and arbitrary world in which nothing existed for her but Fritzs' empire. As it is recounted in the Bible that

Moses was the god of Pharaoh by virtue of the influence he had acquired over the king in changing the water in the cisterns to blood and surrounding him with prodigies, Georges Fritzs became, in a manner of speaking, Pulcherie's god.

However, Fritzs only employed his divinity for the wellbeing of his creature, for Pulcherie was Georges' work; he had been to search for her in the confines of the void, where she was held immobile, in order to drag her toward life by force.

All the secrets that magnetism puts at the disposition of its initiates, all the talismans by which it establishes an intimate and indissoluble commerce between two hearts, were exploited by Georges and Pulcherie to the profit of their amour.

Absent, Georges made use of nature as an intermediary to enable his most secret thoughts to reach Mademoiselle de B***. He attached a virtue of revelation to the benches on which Pulcherie had the habit of sitting, the bushes that bordered the path where she loved to walk, and the sycamores that cast their thick and resinous foliage around her bedroom window.

Everything that existed around Pulcherie talked to her continuously about Georges; creation was no more than a veil covering the invisible and mysterious presence of her lover; the trees, agitating the leaves of their crowns like so many mobile green tongues, were confidants that recounted the ineffable sentiments of the heart that was fond of her; tender things that Fritzs was too modest to say, he communicated to the trees, to the pond, to the flowers and to all of nature; that faint and veiled language alarmed the umbrageous consciousness of the young woman less than speech.

Like ancient magic, magnetism has signs and occult means that aid communication at a distance. Georges and Pulcherie made use of them so as always to be in one another's presence; there was a continual exchange between them of sympathetic ribbons, sachets, locks of hair, medallions, all objects that Georges had, in a sense, consecrated; those talismans exercised on those two strongly united hearts the sweet enchantment of amour.

One evening, when Pulcherie was walking alone in the garden, she saw a rose that attracted her mysteriously; she advanced her hand toward the flower and then approached her face to it, and at the same moment, in the embalmed breath of the rose she drank a mild sleep in which she pronounced Georges' name several times. He had communicated with the rose, in order that Pulcherie would pluck him, and respire him, in a way, in that flower.

XXI

THAT union of Georges and Pulcherie was so intimate, so perfect and so elevated that the two lovers did not think of substituting another for it. Marriage appeared to them to be a crude bond that would add nothing to their happiness. However, people seemed to be occupied with it at the château.

The two lovers had not yet talked about it; Pulcherie was ignorant of the mysteries of marriage and had no understanding of the price that people attach to it. One evening, when they were walking together, arm in arm, in one of the shadiest paths in the park, they were in an ecstasy that exhausted them with joy; it was the moment when melancholy,

Albrecht Dürer's bat,[1] opens its long and trailing wings in the heart to the dubious clarity of twilight. Mademoiselle de B*** was more beautiful than ever; her large dark eyes shone like two nocturnal suns; her cheeks, of a warm and transparent whiteness, were colored by a slight pink cloud; her hand spoke to Fritzs', which she was holding tightly. The two lovers walked, intoxicated by joy, verdure and blue sky, along the narrow path; their lungs inflated superbly and it seemed to them that they were respiring the heavens with every breath of air. Georges Fritzs stopped under the enchanted tree and placed a golden ring on Pulcherie's finger.

"This is our betrothal ring," he told her. "I've attached my soul to it, and for as long as you wear it on your finger, you will love me."

That ring had many other virtues. When Pulcherie wanted to see what the absent Georges was doing she had only to place it

---

1 In the famous engraving *Melencolia* (1514).

on her finger; a clairvoyant sleep immediately moistened her eyelids and the young fiancée could follow with the eyes of her soul the distant footsteps of her lover. There was no retreat, however profound and well-hidden, into which Pulcherie could not slide with that ring, in order to watch Georges' conduct. But for as long as the time of their engagement lasted, while Monsieur de B*** was preparing everything for their marriage at the château, she only ever surprised Fritzs walking alone under the trees, or on the water's edge, with the thought of her in his heart.

XXII

THE château depicted quite well, in its uncultivated and wild condition, the mental state of Mademoiselle de B*** before Georges had opened avenues there in order to enable the daylight to penetrate: it was dark, obstructed and cold. In a short time, a garden and a house take on the character of their owner. The park, especially, had fallen over eight years into a second childhood; the trees were abandoned and tilted sideways, as Pulcherie's stature had been before having been brought upright by Georges; their foliage was entangled with one another; dense, poisonous plants populated by snakes, stifled young bushes, similar to the neural nets in Mademoiselle de B***'s head that had prevented thought from growing. The avenues were cleared, the trees pruned and the listing trunks straightened; for the park and the entire house, as for the young chatelaine, there was a new life.

Joy, movement, noise, festivities and hunting parties had returned for some time; the hoof-beats of horses were heard, dogs shook their previously bleak and bored heads in the courtyards, barking joyfully. Even the domestics changed their livery and their expressions.

Similar work was carried out in the entrance courtyard, which chickens, pigeons and rusty moss had invaded in the masters' absence. The garden, which had devoured the sand of the pathways beneath a crop of weeds, and whose trees had forgotten to produce fruits for a long time, resumed its elegance and its fecundity. Previously, winter and summer had almost resembled one another at the château, so cold, uniform and sad were they, but that year, it seemed that spring returned after a winter that had lasted eight years; swallows, flowers, fruits, leaves, daylight and nature were perceived for the first time. For the entire household, the star conducting that summer was not only the sun.

The same movement was communicated to the Hôtel de B*** in the faubourg Saint-Germain. The noise of pincers and hammers announced to the neighbors the interior labors that had the return of the masters to Paris for a goal. The wall-hangings were renewed; the dusty wheels of the carriages in the courtyard were brushed; the exterior walls of the house were scraped. The old steward of the house, Caleb, seemed rejuvenated in the midst of those preparations, which announced to everyone that the good times of the family de B*** were about to be reborn.

They remained in the country for the entire autumn, however.

For a few weeks, nothing at the château troubled the calm interior wellbeing of that renaissance. Pulcherie's father treated Georges with honor; he introduced him to his friends in the neighborhood, who had returned to the château some time ago, as an extraordinary man from whom one had the right to expect miracles. At table, he sat him to his daughter's right; if wine had been lacking he would gladly have proposed to Georges to make some with water, but Monsieur de B***'s cellar was too well-furnished for that and even the guests of Cana would not have succeeded in drinking it dry.

The magnetic bond that united Georges and Pulcherie was still the same. In encountering one another the two lovers had, in a way completed one another; Mademoiselle de B*** had found a mind in Fritzs, and Fritzs a body, so to speak, in Pulcherie. That positive and real beauty had extracted the young dreamer from his melancholy aspirations in the void, bringing him back to the external life and movement of this world.

They had, therefore, in that rapprochement, rendered one another services mutually, which made them happy. Georges admired himself in Pulcherie; he experienced, in seeing her, the same sentiment of pride and satisfaction that God experienced on the seventh day, when he saw that everything was good, and rested.

XXIII

THE day of rest seemed, in fact, to have arrived for the lovers; they found a perpetual festival in the joy of their hearts. One evening, however, when the family was in the drawing room, occupied in playing cards, Pulcherie descended the steps of the perron lightly. A crescent moon stood out sharply above the somber masses of the park; the perron gave access to a platform on which there were flower-beds and a few benches; Pulcherie had introduced Georges to the milieu of the drawing-room and the young doctor was sitting down waiting for her.

As soon as he saw her coming, he said: "I was calling to you internally, because I needed to see you and to see you alone."

"Why are you weeping?" said Pulcherie, divining a tear in Georges' eyes.

"Because I love you," he replied.

"What! A fine reason for sadness," she said, with a charming smile.

"I wouldn't have any reason for sadness," said Georges, "if there were only us in the world, but . . ."

"Chase away these bad thoughts, then," Mademoiselle de B*** interjected. "You know very well that I love you, and that everything here is done as I wish. I love you, Georges; when we look at one another like this I have your eyes in mine and you have my soul; what you want, I want; what you say, I think.

"I find you handsome, but is that why I love you? I don't believe so. Why, then? I don't know. Loving you is as natural for me, and as necessary, as living. I don't understand myself without you. If I exist, it's because you exist. Before you, I didn't exist; I was waiting for you.

"I needed to say all that! Oh, truly, we love one another, although that word belongs to everyone, and it's necessary to make one for ourselves alone, because other men and women don't have hearts in our image."

As she spoke those words, in a divine voice, Pulcherie parted Fritzs' long hair with her hands and touched his forehead with the edges of her lips.

"Adieu," she said, "I love you."

Then she fled, signaling to him that her duty was to return to the drawing room.

XXIV

GEORGES FRITZS had the beauty that comes from the soul; for the rest, his irregular features, his thinness and the uncultivated abandon of his manner placed him in the category of men that many women do not notice, but whose merit, internal and veiled, in a sense, retains the heart of a lover more than any other.

Some time ago, Pulcherie's interior eyes had opened under the action of magnetism a *second sight*, which penetrated the obscure night of the future. She had presentiments that were never mistaken. Her mind discovered in slumber the fugitive and luminous traces of events not yet accomplished, which she imparted to Fritzs.

One morning, when the cool night air was blowing its last breezes through the foliage of the park, Pulcherie told Georges about a dream that she had had during the night.

"I dreamed," she said to him, "that the two of us were chatting on the balcony; we were cheerful and happy, as we are now. A fresh wind, charged with the breath of flowers, was entering lightly into the drawing room, agitating its curtains. While we were chatting foolishly, holding hands, we heard three raps on the door. We looked at one another with a muted anxiety. Those three blows had struck our hearts; we had not heard them, we had understood them. The door opened of its own accord. The being that entered was me, or, rather, it was my specter, for I saw that I was pale, livid and bleak, facing myself. That specter advanced on to the balcony where we were taking the air and called to me, by name, three times. Fear gripped me, and I woke up."

"That's a terrible dream," Georges remarked.

"Terrible, indeed," said Pulcherie. "Is not that double being, all that gaiety on one side and all that pallor on the other, that living being confronting its shadow, something to awaken somber presentiments?"

"Are you quite sure," George insisted, "that the specter was yours?"

"Yes, I recognized myself; the specter had my features, my gaze and my voice, except that it was, as I told you, much paler than me; I shall doubtless resemble it when I am dead."

After having walked for some time in silence, Georges and Pulcherie returned sadly to the château.

XXV

FOR several days, Monsieur de B*** had been colder than usual with regard to Georges; he seemed to want to reestablish between him and his daughter a distance that the young doctor had suddenly crossed.

The comte was a nobleman very much in keeping with the blazon, who could not resign himself to relegate among the vague relics of old times the parchments and titles that had cost his ancestors so dear. He owed a great deal to Monsieur Fritzs and he remembered that. He was a man of honor who had never wanted to remain backward in recognizing a service, and Fritz had rights to the hand of Pulcherie, but the comte's duty in that circumstance seemed to him to be hard to keep, now that the most proven gentlemen of France were seeking the honor of such a marriage on their knees. The name was illustrious, the bride accomplished, and perhaps he wanted Fritzs, without admitting it very clearly to himself, to understand that embarrassment of the head of an ancient family, and withdraw gradually from a union mismatched in the eyes of society.

Georges Fritzs was a young philosopher who bore in his heart all the pride of a scholar and all the delicacy of an honest man. Veiled as it was, he understood the comte's intimate thought; he was wounded by it; his heart bled for a long time in the milieu of the calm and silence of the fields.

Horrible as the sacrifice was for him, who could not live without Pulcherie, he tried to detach himself from his amour, but he could not succeed in doing so; the more he tried to separate himself from her, the more she became entwined with him, like ivy. For Georges, Pulcherie was one of those human creations that the ancient alchemists claimed to obtain by means of the secrets of science, which then pursued them throughout life.

Georges had, moreover, firstly, a heart caught in Pulcherie's; he could no longer disengage his thought from the visible beauty that had made it descend from the cloudy heights of dream to the calm and grandiose lines of nature. Those two individuals were joined to one another by an inevitable and sweet need, like lips to a cup; to divide them was to want their doom. Nevertheless, Georges Fritzs was led, by an extravagant generosity, to an abrupt and sudden resolution that had a decisive influence on their destinies.

XXVI

ONE morning, when she awoke, Mademoiselle de B*** drew apart the curtains of her bed in order to allow the first rays of the sun to arrive at her eyes. It was the month of August; all of nature was saluting the rebirth of daylight with birdsong and the flutter of wings. A clematis was swaying its white stars over the window, within tufts of verdure. Pulcherie mingled her heart internally with the morning festivity. A fresh breeze brought the dew of the park over her windows in odorous pearls. She woke up joyfully; nothing in the world is sweeter than the accord of the pure heart of a young woman with the dawn of a beautiful day.

Having chanced to glance at her night-table however, Mademoiselle de B*** found a letter there; she opened it. The letter was addressed to her in Georges' handwriting:

I am departing; I am ordered to do so by an old uncle who wants to embrace me before dying; I am going to Switzerland.

Adieu, you whom I love more than any woman was ever loved.

Georges Fritzs.

Mademoiselle de B*** got up, dressed in haste and went out in utter disorder to stop Georges' flight. She interrogated her servants, who told her that they had not heard anything. They went to the young doctor's room but found it empty. Hoof-prints in the sand of the second courtyard enabled belief in a nocturnal escape. Minute precautions had been taken to quieten the barking of the guard dogs.

A courier was sent along the road that the traveler seemed to have taken, but no trace of him could be found. It was then presumed that he had forced his horse to cross a small river that blocked the passage on one side of the château, in order to put any pursuit off the track.

Mademoiselle de B*** was seized by an anguish impossible to describe; her sighs choked her; it was necessary to put her to bed, where she did not take long to be gripped by a bad fever.

In her delirium she repeated Georges' name a thousand times.

XXVII

AFTER a few days the fever calmed down, but it left Mademoiselle de B*** in a state of depression more to be feared than the violence of the malady. The absence of Georges had a mortal effect on her; she fell into a slack languor, something in her had departed with the man she loved; the warmth of life was suddenly lacking in her; she had lost in her lover the star of her soul and she became, in less than a week, what the flowers of the fields would become if the sun ceased to shine.

Convalescent for several months, she was gradually gripped again by the terrible mental illness from which Georges Fritzs had extracted her. Her mind was distant, with the young doctor; her heart had departed with her lover.

Day by day she became what she had been before, a poor insensible creature close to the void, whom an amorous breath had brought briefly to life.

She only recovered a little clairvoyance and reason when the ring of which Fritzs had made her a gift was put on her finger. That ring, which was gold, very simply wrought, enabled her to follow her absent friend with the eyes of her heart; she saw him then as if he were with her.

"He's thinking about me," she often said. "We're walking together on the edge of a lake, over which large white birds are flying. We still love one another, my beloved and I!"

She found so much melancholy and sweetness in those moments of ecstasy spent with the absent Georges that she wept when, for fear of fatigue, the ring was taken away from her. That enchanted ring brought her closer to the author of the principle of her life; it was the ring of a mystical and supernatural alliance, at which hearts sometimes arrive on earth when their thoughts and their amour are already—prior to them, as it were—in heaven.

When she ceased to see Georges it seemed that a great night fell upon her heart. Her pretty head, weighed down by slumber, tilted like a poppy on its stem. She fell back then into the former torpor, into the death of the soul from which Georges had resuscitated her. Without him, she was no longer good for anything but sleeping and being beautiful.

Her health, previously so strong, began to deteriorate again; the freshness of her complexion was tarnished; the roses of her mouth shed their petals; everything in her was perishing. Pulcherie went away with the autumn, with the last flocks of wild doves that passed before the windows of the château.

XXVIII

THE mental state of Georges Fritzs was scarcely less alarming. Retired to a chalet in Switzerland, he watched sadly, during the pale days of autumn, the death of nature and that of his heart.

His amour had been born in spring with the green leaves, and it fell with them. The young doctor could not withdraw his thought from Pulcherie's. He wept while walking alone in the depths of uncultivated woods that reminded him of the forests of the Berri. He fell ill with homesickness, for our homeland is not where we were born but where the woman we love is.

He had tried hard to rid himself of that amour, but he soon recognized that it would be easier to rid himself of his life. He therefore resigned himself to dying gradually, in order that the mad passion might die with him and that Comte de B*** would then recover all liberty with regard to his daughter's hand.

Such was the fate of Georges and Pulcherie. They had, so to speak, the malady of one another. It was necessary, at all costs, to bring them together again or to see them die.

The comte was a father. He had been able to yield to excusable prejudices and lend too complaisant an ear to what is called the honor of a family, but he loved his daughter and, seeing her fall back into such a deplorable state, he wrote to Monsieur Fritzs begging him to come back in all haste.

XXIX

GEORGES came back. Pulcherie was re-animated as he came closer. She divined him more than thirty leagues away. When he came in, it was a celestial joy for her; their discolored lips sought one another for a long time in a pale kiss that had the chill and chastity of death.

For a few days, Mademoiselle de B*** recovered all her mental health; her mind and her heart had returned with Georges; but her constitution, weakened by the malady of his absence, retained ineffable traces of exhaustion. The gleam that her eyes acquired at the sight of the young doctor was that of a dying lamp that is reanimated momentarily before being extinguished completely.

The two lovers were beset by sinister presentiments. The first snow that fell on the ground seemed to them to be a white shroud that would cover both of them. The voice of the crows under the gray sky threw a heart-rending sadness into the soul. They walked in a melancholy manner, to the sound of the wind in the branches, dragging dead leaves underfoot, along the solitary paths of the park.

"We are the fiancés of death." Pulcherie said to Georges, putting her hand in his. "Our marriage bed will be a lead coffin, and my bridal crown a crown of white immortelles. What does it matter? We shall not quit one another in the other world any more than in this one, and even death will not be strong enough to disunite us."

Pulcherie and Georges retained all their knowledge until the last moment. They understood one another with a glance and a squeeze of the hand. They almost had no need of speech in order to converse with one another, so united were their souls.

XXX

ONE morning, Pulcherie awoke with a strange gaze in her eyes. She ordered her women to dress her in her bed. She organized her toilette herself: a white dress, a veil and a crown of orange-blossom in her hair. When she was ready, Mademoiselle de B*** asked for her father. He came in great haste. When he came in, Pulcherie raised herself up on her elbow, took her father's hand in hers, and said to him respectfully: "Will you lead me to the altar, Monsieur le Comte?"

Thinking that his daughter was delirious, Monsieur de B*** urged her to calm down, but Pulcherie insisted on asking for a priest. Her request was granted and the village curé came to her sickbed in a white surplice and a violet stole, with the holy oils.

"You're mistaken," said Pulcherie, with a charming smile. "It isn't extreme unction that you're going to perform, but a marriage . . ."

Then looking toward the door, she added: "My husband is very late."

At the same instant, Georges appeared. He was very pale; his arm leaning on that of a domestic, he advanced slowly. The eyes of the spectators wandered sadly from the melancholy figure of the young man to Pulcherie's deathbed.

Then the young woman bid adieu to her mother, her father and the entire household, saying that she was going to the eternal wedding. "Don't weep," she added, "for my fiancé is mine and I am his."

There was, however, much weeping around her bed.

The priest performed all the ceremonies of the marriage. When he asked the comte for his consent, the poor father did not reply; he dissolved in tears. Pulcherie and Georges were the only ones who were calm. The serenity of heaven shone in their eyes; Pulcherie had never been so beautiful; paradise was divinable behind the holy and transparent pallor of virginity. She followed the prayers of the church attentively; the pall was extended over the heads of the two spouses and the priest, having blessed the magnetized ring, gave it to Georges in order for him to place it on Pulcherie's finger.

"This ring," she said then, "will enable me to follow all my beloved's thoughts in heaven. I want it to be left on my finger when I am dead."

When the priest had completed the last rites of the marriage, she turned to the comte and added: "Permit me now, Father, to go with my husband."

At the same instant, Georges having got up from the armchair in which he had remained seated by virtue of weakness throughout the ceremony, threw himself into Pulcherie's arms; their hearts touched with a supreme beat, and their two mouths were confounded in the same last sigh. Georges doubtless received the soul of his beloved then, and bore it away to heaven.

XXXI

THE two lovers were buried under the same stone in the park of the château. Their names were inscribed thereon. I have seen that simple and touching monument, which encloses one of the greatest secrets of the human heart. A hawthorn branch hangs above it, charged with dew, and alongside it, two little birds sing the symphonies of the Unknown.

Physicians have been unable to give any explanation of the strange malady that they were unable to cure. Pulcherie's entire life, like Georges', has remained a mystery for science. It is therefore necessary to seek an explanation higher up.

Poetry knows the last word of everything, and it is to her that it is fitting to raise around the soul the thick veils that the hand of Mesmer and Hoffmann has already tried to uncover.

Mademoiselle de B***, after having lived for some time in her fiancé, after having united her heart with that of Fritzs by indivisible bonds, as Antonia united her soul with the strings of Krespel's violin,[1] was extinguished with the failing young doctor and died in the man she had loved.

---

1 In the story by Hoffmann originally entitled "Rat [or Rath] Krespel" (1819; tr. in English as "Councillor Krespel" or "The Cremona Violin"). It is nowadays best known for its dramatization in Jacques Offenbach's opera *Les Contes of Hoffmann* (1880).

EBN
SINA

I

EBN SINA[1] was an old alchemist of the fifteenth century who sought, like Geber, the universal remedy, and the method of making gold, like Raymond Lull. Old histories attribute the honor of the discovery of that science to the first angels, who were supposed to have been amorous of the first women; the story is not very gallant, since, according to it, even the angels would have needed to have recourse with women to a certain gift in order to make themselves welcome; but that

---

1 This name is an obvious appropriation of that of Ibn Sina (c980-1037), the great Persian physician and polymath known in the West as Avicenna, but the character in the story bears no resemblance to the actual Ibn Sina.

fable was not invented yesterday, and nothing prevents us from thinking that women have changed considerably since those times.

Throughout his life, which had been long and turbulent, Ebn Sina had only ever had one passion, which was science. Like all mistresses that are courted too ardently, however, science had shown herself to be completely intractable. He was reaching his eighty-third year and he had never spent a day without leafing through his books and lighting his furnace; more than five heritages and a few considerable legacies had disappeared in turn in ruinous experiments; flame had worn away its tongue licking the contours of the crucible; the bellows had no more breath, and still the operation that advertised itself as rich in gold only give birth to a little ash.

No other patience would have held firm, but instead of breaking his furnaces and disemboweling his old asthmatic bellows, the scholar, after a vain experiment, tranquilly postponed success until tomorrow. Nothing disconcerted that faith, as old and unbreakable as rock. Every day Ebn Sina invented new methods, and as those methods were always found in default, the scholar concluded that it was necessary to begin again.

Meanwhile, a certain odor, described in the books, escaped the ardent crucible in the middle of his operations, and announced to him that he was on the track of his discovery. Ebn Sina became old and ill, but he continued his attempts nevertheless; the fire would become weary of burning sooner than he would weary of blowing.

For several days, however, the scholar seemed to have been plunged in an absorbing meditation; his disciple Emmaus, a young man seventeen years old, with a brow already pensive and silky blond hair, no longer dared to interrupt that formidable silence, which had to be brooding some great creation. Emmaus was one of those handsome adolescents who attach themselves to some aged hermetic scientist in order to take care of him and to be initiated under his direction into the secrets of the *magister*. Melancholy and mild, with eyes the color of the sky, the disciple composed poetry while sitting on a stool in the venerable hovel of science. His pretty head leaned gravely on his hand and formed with the severe head of Ebn Sina, lying horizontally on a mattress extended on the ground, a contrast full of grace.

The old man was thinking, the child dreaming. Nothing was heard in the humble cell but the intermittent sound of their breathing and the murmur of folios stirred by the wind. Sometimes, a bird came to perch on the window, open in the fashion of a skylight near the ceiling, with a grille of iron bars corroded by rust. Emmaus lifted his head then, but the old man did not hear it.

Ebn Sina was in the state of mental enchantment that a Greek artist has depicted on a bas-relief by representing Jupiter with a sober expression, whose forehead Vulcan has just struck with a hammer.

Ebn Sina had never gone so long without putting his hand on his instruments; the round-bellied flasks, the alembics with slender and tapering necks like those of storks, and the curved madrases seemed to be astonished and to lament that abandonment. The furnace, which had fasted for a week, opened its empty maw in a corner. The bellows crouching in the middle of the room no longer gave any sign of life. Every day dust descended on the earthenware jars; a little more, and spiders would have spun webs there.

"What is the master doing?" the cold crucibles seemed to be saying. "Has he renounced his dreams of potable gold? What was the point, then, in wearing away our flanks with the bites of flame? If the science is only a chimera, let him say so and let us take our leave! He will not be the first, then, to extract gold from the vein of molten metals and who will make of that friable gold and elixir whose effect is to postpone death for more than a thousand years? Courage, Master! Get up!

Take care that death does not come to surprise you before you become immortal; hurry up and become a god."

There were such mysterious relationships between that family of chemical instruments and the paternal heart of the scholar that the reader ought not to be surprised if the flasks, the furnace and the crucibles took the liberty of addressing speech to him.

One day, when he woke up, Emmaus saw a ray of June sunlight descending between the bars of the skylight, which summoned him outside; the sky was blue and the soul of the spring that rejuvenates the world was tangible in the air. The disciple darted a glance at his master. Ebn Sina was still in the contemplative and reflective position that the statues lying on the marble tombs in our churches have. Emmaus got up quietly and, after having adjusted his garments, opened the door gently and went out.

Left alone, the scholar did not appear to perceive Emmaus' absence, but after a few moments of silence and immobility he raised himself up on his elbow and, putting his chilly hands together he said: "The daylight is bright today." Then, turning to the Orient with a solemn air, he added: "Spirit of Solomon and great Hermes, inspire me! Have pity on the last of your sons, who has sown mercury in the fields of Gomorrah and whose wizened hands have only ever harvested ashes. Enable your servant, before dying, to see the salvation that you have prepared for the children of science. And you, Sun, universal fire, soul of nature, principal of all metals, allow to fall from the long lashes of your eyelids a single one of your rays, to fecundate my virgin crucible today!"

According to the ancient hermetic scientists, gold is sunlight in the solid state.

Having said that, he stood up and washed his hands carefully in an earthenware vase; the science is a jealous and simple divinity that one ought only to approach with clean hands. Then, loading his furnace with charcoal, Ebn Sina addressed it in these terms:

"And you, furnace, recipient of the fire that is the secret agent of nature, Vulcan with the lame foot, I adjure you by Averroes and Mithra, the two princes, to do your duty. Burn, my son, and remember the fortunate furnace of Ab Selamim,[1] which, for having perfected the Great Work, remained lit for a thousand years!"

We cannot say whether the furnace was sensible to that exhortation, but the truth is that it did not take long to catch fire. Ebs Sina did not spare, to that effect, the short and unequal breath of the old bellows, which had resumed its service in the scholar's hands When the incandescent surface of the furnace permitted him to apply the crucible to it, the old man sat beside it on a stool, with the solicitude of a surgeon watching over a woman in labor. In Ebn Sina's mind, the crucible was pregnant with gold, but the poor instrument had already had so many stillbirths that it could not be watched too carefully.

---

1 Selamim is a Hebrew term meaning "peace-offering," or "sacrifice."

It was a grave and singular spectacle, worthy of the pencil of Rembrandt: the scholar in that somber cell, his face illuminated by the glow of the brazier. The deep wrinkles on his bald forehead stood out rigid and dense, like the creases of his lips, folded in parchment. His head was titled forward and his eyes were covering with mute attention the molten metals.

For that man, at that moment, there was no sun, no spring and no nature; the birds sang in vain over his head and the gentle waves of the Seine kissed in vain with a soft sound the strand inundated with strollers; his sun was his lighted furnace. A cloud of thick black smoke rose furiously from the crucible and spread a suffocating odor throughout the cell, which drew a dry cough, tenacious and hoarse, from the old man's lungs several times over. But what did that cough matter to him, who could already glimpse immortality through the fumes of the crucible and the darkness of the science?

At each precipitation, every time the substance in labor quit its primitive color to take on a new one—which the ancient alchemists designated by the name of metamorphoses—the face of the scholar brightened with hope. Already the *corbeau* had changed into the *colombe* and the *colombe* into the *épervier*; which is to say that the contents had passed from black to white and from white to yellow. The experiment was on the way to success. All the characteristics furnished by the book to announce the preliminaries of the transmutation had been produced; Ebn Sina was definitely on the path, this time, to the great arcanum.

Meanwhile, the moment for the final precipitate had come. Ebn Sina reanimated the force of the furnace by giving it a further ration of fuel to devour. Then, seizing the bellows and compressing it violently, he said: "Blow, my old soul, blow! We're approaching the solemn moment; we're about to make gold. You will be greater than the god Aeolus, the great ventilator, whose exploits were celebrated by the poet Virgilius in his book."

The bellows, doubtless flattered by that comparison, filled its cheeks with air and emptied them impetuously over the charcoal in the furnace, the combustion of which it stimulated. An acidic vapor spread through the room, but the scholar paid no heed to it. Having done that, he charged the ardent and hissing crucible with new substances, which foamed as it worked like a charger. The bellows continued to spur on the flame, entirely out of breath, but its master said: "Courage, my friend; hold firm; we're about to reach the terminus."

O miracle! A reddish powder, the true projection powder described by the ancient alchemists—it was impossible to doubt its color—escaped from the crucible in a fine and friable rain. At that sight, Ebn Sina, seized by a lyrical transport of which he could not moderate the shocks or the surges, said:

"Oh! Gold! Here's the gold! A little of that powder in water and I shall be immortal for at least a thousand years! The world is mine! I shall found cities and buy women. Have you not done well, Ebn Sina, to keep your heart apart until now from the pleasures and passions of the crowd? When you were young, old scholar, while you withered away deciphering the pages of the grimoire, the world laughed, danced and feasted around you. It's your turn now! You shall be adored; you shall be a king.

"You will travel to the Orient, to the land of the magi, where pearls emerge white and mat from the bosom of the sea, where the sun warms and the women are beautiful. You will build a palace that will make Solomon's forgotten; the Queen of Sheba will come to visit you from the extremities of the earth, and all peoples will prostrate themselves before your face. Rejoice!

"Gold is, in any case, only a symbol; this crucible is only an image of the great crucible in which you will melt the entire world. You will change and transmute nations. Gold is glory. You will shine like Moses, the great alchemist, who had received the science of the Egyptians and who bore two horns of light on his head. Henceforth, the science is your vassal and your servant; all those figures of mystery, Isis, Mithra and Osiris, who hide so obstinately from other mortals, will let their veils fall before you. With your gold you will forge a key that will unlock all the secrets of nature. O Ebn Sna, bless the star under which you were born!"

The scholar tried to get up, but his head was heavy. The chamber was full of carbon vapor, for Ebn Sina had forgotten to open the window of the skylight. Three times he tried to drag himself to the door and three times he fell back on to the stool, stiff, nailed to the spot; his stiff and wrinkled hands extended toward the furnace in order to bring back to the edge a little of the powder that enabled one to live for a thousand years, but they could not reach it. A cloud extended over his eyes, his tongue stuck to his palate, and he felt himself becoming as hard as stone.

II

MEANWHILE, Emmaus, the beloved
disciple, had been to refresh his lungs,
burned by sulfur and carbon, with the air of
a spring day. He came back along the Seine
cheerfully. Emmaus was more of a poet than
a scholar by nature. He had studied alchemy
because of the beautiful blue figures height-
ened with gold that his fingers encountered
with delight on the pages of the grimoire. He
loved the myths of the science, Orpheus torn
apart by the bacchantes, and the fire of heaven
stolen by Prometheus. Often, he still told himself that it was better to surprise the secrets of
nature in herself than to pursue them sadly in
the gloom of a laboratory. He took pleasure
among trees and liked the sunlight. In the

evening hours when, like women vanquished by the heat of the day, nature become more confident and more communicative, Emmaus liked to interrogate her in the depths of woods or on the banks of rivers.

This evening, the sun, having descended behind the city, red and incandescent, resembled an immense furnace over which the somber mass of houses was posed like an alchemist's crucible. Emmaus stopped. He said to himself that perhaps the dreams of hermetic science were like the horizon of solid gold that was about to be extinguished and vanish. The disciple even wondered internally whether the hectic research of material wealth was worthy of a man. His mind hesitated as to whether he ought not to detach himself from his covetousness in order to elevate himself to nobler designs.

"Instead of tormenting matter in every direction," he exclaimed, "in order to extract a little gold from it, might I not do better—might we not do better, O Ebn Sina—to devote the faculties that God has entrusted to us to informing our fellows and discovering the great secret of intelligences? Even if the philosophers' stone is not a chimera, even if you are on the point of discovering it, Master, do you not think, as I do, that it would be better to civilize men than to transform metals and brute substances? I prefer a kind thought to all the gold of which you dream."

Emmaus lingered for a few more minutes on the quay watching a window obscured by curtains. The disciple had amours more human than his master. The window was that of Thérèse, a beautiful young woman of eighteen who sometimes took the air on her balcony in the evening. Emmaus loved Thérèse and was loved by her, but the young woman had the misfortune of being rich, and like the disciple, she was counting a great deal on the science of Ebn Sina to facilitate their union.

That evening Thérèse did not appear on her balcony; Emmaus only saw a light shadow outlined on the mist of the curtains, which blew him a kiss with its hand.

The disciple returned to his master's dwelling at sunset. His young head was full of dreams of amour and poetry; he stopped for a moment to collect himself before going back into the obscure sanctuary of the science.

Ebn Sina's house was bizarre and tall; a roof opened out in the middle in a sort of terrace permitting the course of the constellations to be followed from there; a chimney with a long neck ordinarily discharged thick smoke into the sky in intermittent gusts that resemble the respiration of a volcano, but this evening no serpent of fumes unwound its fleecy coils over the starry transparency of the sky. Night had fallen; the quays, surprised by the warm and emollient obscurity of a spring evening, wound their sinuous lines silently, over which the line of the houses could scarcely be seen any longer.

The curfew had rung. Emmaus therefore decided to go back into the old scholar's tower; he climbed the steep spiral staircase, plunged obscurely in its stone cylinder, with a light step. Having arrived at the door of the cell, the disciple put his ear to the disjointed planks that sealed the entrance; he could not hear any sound, not even the light murmur that the wind rendered as it was engulfed by the skylight. He concluded that Ebn Sina was asleep and opened the door to the room cautiously.

It was very dark. A ray of moonlight illuminated coldly the face of the scholar, lying on the floor. Emmaus contemplated him silently. His master still had the same attitude of profound and blissful meditation in which he had left him that morning. As Emmaus was an artist, he paused for a few moments to follow with an attentive eye the strong and severe lines that designed the configuration of that remarkable head.

The scholar was lying on his back; his hands, folded over his breast, seemed weary of trying to grasp the void; a white beard descended in thick waves from his chin; his forehead was tilted forward, drawn by the weight of the head and his staring eyes seemed to be studying an object that was standing out confusedly before him in the darkness.

Emmaus lit a wax candle. On following the direction of the gaze that the scholar was attaching to the floor he discovered an extinct furnace charged with a cold and empty crucible, which designed an exaggerated shadow on the wall.

Oh, he said to himself, *the master has blown today; the acrid and caustic vapor spread through the room is perceptible.*

At the same time he opened the window of the skylight to let in some air, which caused the light of a group of stars to enter the cell.

Meanwhile, Emmaus tried to interrogate at closer range the results of the chemical experiment that appeared to him, at first, to be like all the others, only having ended up swelling the volume of ash with which Ebn Sina enriched himself every day, with a persevering joy. The instruments were in the disorder of an interrupted action. The forceps extended their immobile fingers next to the extinct furnace. The flat and collapsed bellows were lying on the floor on the other side. Flasks and metal debris strewn on a table announced an endeavor completed; the crucible was empty.

O surprise, however! By the vacillating light of the candle, the disciple distinguished around the furnace a light red powder that his master had once mentioned to him, and which, according to learned alchemists, must be projection powder.

At that sight, Emmaus went pale with joy, and, accumulating on the floor a fine and ideal pinch of that dust, he rubbed a copper coin with it; the coin became gold.

"My master has found it!" cried Emmaus, putting his hands together with intoxication.

Then, holding his breath for fear of blowing away the admirable dust, Emmaus began to consider it silently.

"You are great," he said, turning toward Ebn Sina. "You will reign for a thousand years, like Methuselah, and you will be adored like the god Baal. Master, have pity on your disciple, who is not even worthy to untie the laces of your sandals. His heart, young and carnal, is not, like yours, purified of the weaknesses of nature. While you were making gold, O incomparable one, he was picking flowers by the roadside and gazing at the radiance in the foliage. Do not show him for that a severe face, O Ebn Sina; he is not, like you, a solid and positive mind able to watch over a furnace for forty years. Being rich, have pity on the poet!

"We shall be happy, Thérèse and I; I shall sew diamonds in her dress; I shall attach solid gold bracelets to her wrists, so fine that they will be mistaken for the coils of a snake. We shall have slaves and marble baths! Bring us flowers! The walls of our palace will be covered with paintings and bas-reliefs, like the walls of a cathedral.

"To work, master! Here I am; let us recommence the experiment. Is it necessary to re-light the furnace? Is it necessary to blow? Let's spend the night making gold. Tomorrow, we'll be richer than the king of France. I am at your orders, Ebn Sina. If you no longer have the strength to shift the instruments or precipitate the substances, indicate them to me and I will carry out your instructions. One word, and we are masters of the world. You have vanquished the Sphinx, Ebn Sina; you have extracted from the bronze mouth the fatal word of the enigma; repeat that word to me.

"Come on, what is it necessary to do? I'm waiting. You can reflect another day, Master; but today time is pressing. Take care that your memory doesn't fail; let's make haste, let's make haste."

Seeing that Ebn Sina made no sign or gave any response, Emmaus, struck by a horrible presentiment, passed the flame of the candle before the scholar's lips; it did not stir.

"Ebn Sina! Ebn Sina!" cried the young man, in a desperate voice, into his master's ears. The master did not raise his eyes.

Then the disciple touched his master's hands; they were cold.

"Dead!" said the distressed disciple. "And the secret?" he thought, aloud. "Who will tell me the secret? The furnace and the crucible are still here, but they have both forgotten it. The walls are mute; and this old man . . ."

Beside himself, Emmaus started shaking the scholar's cadaver furiously.

"Speak, then, dead man!"

The scholar's head, agitated by his hand, made a formidable movement, but soon resumed its center of gravity on the breast.

Emmaus ran around the room like a madman, imploring all the objects with his gaze to speak to him, collecting the powder strewn in the ground in tiny quantity in order to submit it to analysis. In fact, he reanimated the extinct furnace and tried the virtue of solvents in order to lay bare the substances contained in the projection powder; but all his efforts failed; the powder evaporated under the action of heat; all his gold went up in smoke.

The mystery, which had emerged momentarily from the murky profundities of nature, had returned there, perhaps forever. The scholar was dead, and his secret had died with him. Emmaus had questioned the crucible and the old man in vain; the one responded by devouring the last traces of the victory, the other, his mouth irrevocably closed and his jaws clenched, imitated the silence of statues; science had taken back its secret.

Emmaus could not determine himself, however, to release the wings of the gilded chimera that he had held in his hand a little while ago. He returned impetuously to the old man.

"The secret, Master! Tell me the secret! You're not dead, are you? Haven't mages been seen, in any case, to sit up in their tombs in order to instruct the living? Theodose de Meun, having been buried with an incomplete manuscript that contained, under cabalistic figures, the secrets of magistery, continued his work after his death; and when his tomb was opened, after half a century, the blank pages were found to be covered with writing and images. Can you not come back, great Ebn Sina, you who have vanquished the mystery of nature? Can you not slide the key to the enigma into the ear of your disciple? I won't confide it to anyone, Master, I swear to you. The science has killed you in order to punish you for having violated its secrets; try to grasp the expression of them with your cold lips; avenge yourself! One word, Master; speak! Speak!"

Emmaus accompanied these arguments with a flask of an alkali, from which he disengaged corrosive scents into the flared nostrils of the scholar.

Ebn Sina slowly closed his eyes, reopened them, paraded around him a stupid and dull gaze, and then fell back into his inexorable silence.

"You're alive!" cried Emmaus, transported. "You're alive, Master! We're saved! Make an effort, Ebn Sina! Try to unclench your stony jaws; one gesture, and I'll understand; give me a sign, and I'll remake for you the elixir that cures death."

The disciple presented the flask again to the old man's nose, but this time Ebn Sina did not make any movement; he was asleep forever.

Emmaus was devastated, and maintained silence, but eventually he turned toward the scholar's crucible and utensils.

"Adieu," he said; "I'm quitting you forever. The goal of our ambitions was immoral; heaven has reckoned with Ebn Sina and me as a punishment. By dint of pursuing the progress of chemical substances, we had lost sight of the development of our nature. Like that bellows, which uses its breath against flame, we only aspired to perishable treasures and we blew to fatigue the elements. A truce! Mind, virtue, intelligence, I'm returning to you; I'm returning to more durable riches; receive a disciple who repents and is breaking his earthenware idols today!"

Emmaus crushed the scholar's crucible underfoot.

"Insensates that we were," Emmaus continued, "to believe that all progress was material and to seek human grandeur therein! That wealth is only an illusion; it's a wealth of the poor, for the true wealth resides in the depths of the mind and the heart. If the science of gold ever penetrated into societies, it would become an incurable poison there, and sick humankind would only be cured, like me, by a return toward justice and conscience."

CPSIA information can be obtained
at www.ICGtesting.com
Printed in the USA
FSHW011539030221
78189FS